About the Author

I've always loved to write and kept journals from an early age. Addicted to drama and excitement, I wanted to be a journalist, travelling all over the world to report the news. With a degree in psychology, two children and a failed marriage behind me, I started to share my adventures on social media, which led to my first book, *A Year of Tiramisu*. I still see life as a series of (mis)adventures, but I'm very serious about writing. *A Year of SINatra* continues my story.

A Year of SINatra

L.J. Brown

A Year of SINatra

Chimera

CHIMERA PAPERBACK

© Copyright 2020
L.J. Brown

A CIP catalogue record for this title is
available from the British Library.

ISBN 978 1 903136 68 3

Chimera is an imprint of
Pegasus Elliot MacKenzie Publishers Ltd.
www.pegasuspublishers.com

First Published in 2020

Chimera
**Sheraton House Castle Park
Cambridge England**

Printed & Bound in Great Britain

Dedication

To the BBC for the radio interview and continued support and to my publisher for your patience.

To Amy, we have been on quite a journey together, my darling friend. Thank you for being my eyes when sometimes I couldn't see.

To Mr. Seattle, I think you are my biggest fan. Thank you for your support and for teaching me that the word "knickers" in America is NOT sexy. It will always be about the panties from now on...

To Doctor Phillip, for your legal guidance, financial support and always looking after me.

To Sinatra, for your beautiful songs, I found so much meaning in your words.

To Wusan and twenty years of friendship, what happens in Narnia stays in Narnia.

And finally, to the Silver Fox, always remember us this way.

Preface

What a year! So, let's have a recap. I'd left my husband, pretty much had a complete mental breakdown, fucked up all my finances and almost got arrested, by the same police officer, for flashing in public twice. I had had a rebound love affair with Mr. Fancy Pants, messed everything up and had hit rock bottom.

In these very hard depressing times of having nothing and being no one, the diary I had kept over the first year of my separation turned into an extremely naughty, controversial book called A Year of Tiramisu.

Yes, of course Mr. Fancy Pants and I remained in contact, but in his predictable absence I was chased by a sexy Silver Fox and quite happily let myself become his dinner.

This rollercoaster year of sexual exploration and self-discovery takes you to a new world of shocking encounters and breath-taking drama.

All aboard the crazy train, next stop's the big dipper... and don't you dare close your eyes.

Contents

Chapter One:
New York, New York

Darkness was everywhere. Where the fuck was I? What was going on? I could hear very loud footsteps in the distance coming towards me; the sound echoed around the room, magnifying the intensity, getting louder and louder on approach. "Hello, who's there?" The footsteps stopped for a minute, then started again. I was completely frozen to the spot in terror. "Please, I'm scared. Put a light on and show yourself to me?" The footsteps stopped again and then picked up speed, running, banging on the floor with deafening volume. I was absolutely petrified, trying to scream, but no sound would come out of my mouth. My heart beating at a million miles an hour in my ear, I couldn't breathe, I couldn't move; then there was deadly silence.

"BOO!"

I tried to scream out loud and bolt, but my feet were glued to the spot. "Who is it?" I yelped in terror and confusion.

"It's me!"

My heart then bounced back to life at the sound

of his voice and I instantly stopped shaking and became cross and confused. "You fucking assehole, that just scared the shit out of me!" I paused and then tried to reach out to him in the darkness to punch him but couldn't see where he was.

"I know it was hilarious; you'll have to let me do that again sometime."

"Let you do it again? Do you think I'm having fun here? Are you crazy?" I snapped.

"Well, this is your dream, so you're controlling what's happening." I could almost feel the smugness in his sarcastic tone.

"I'm dreaming?"

"Yes, you are. Can we hurry this up? I have a date ..."

"I didn't invite you here. I'm trying to make sure you go away and never come back again, so you can just leave." Oh my, I must have been thinking about him again. Come on, L.J., think about someone else and hopeful he will go away.

"I'm the one in control of your heart remember. You don't know how to get me to go away. I win until you're over me." he said very matter of fact. I could hear his satisfaction and feel his devilish smirk, he loved it that he had all this power over me.

"No, you are not. You have lost ALL control and I'm not yours anymore. Leave this dream and leave my mind. You're like an evil spirit; be gone you demon!" I crossed my arms and stood tall in the darkness.

The light flicked on, startling me, blinding my eyes. He was stood right in front of me, as close as he could get to my face. I looked at him, his thick, jet-black hair and perfect white teeth, expressionless, he was just looking at me with his burning hazel eyes. Then he stepped forward and leaned towards my face to kiss me. I closed my eyes in anticipation and leaned forward to meet his lips. "Got you again! Ha... you don't want me to go at all; you're still completely in love with me." He shrugged his shoulders and took a few paces back, giving me jazz hands.

"What the fuck! What are you doing? Just go, you, totals assehole, I hate you!" My face was burning red with anger and embarrassment and I clenched my fists.

"Yes, I am an assehole," he said with complete conviction. He then smiled at me and slowly walked towards me again. I tried to take a step back but I was still glued to the spot. "Make me go then L.J!" giving me a look of devilment he waited for my response.

"What as in fight you?" I was confused for a minute. Was he joking? "You'll have to let my legs move; I'm stuck to the spot!" He looked at my feet and told me to try to move them, and they were suddenly free. "Okay... Choose a weapon, Fancy

Pants. I'm going to kick your ass! I got up to his face this time and pushed my forehead against his, meeting his eyes with a glare that I never knew I had.

"I will choose both our weapons; if you feel you are certain you will win, then it won't matter what we fight with, will it?"

"Okay, deal." I looked at him and scowled. I will get you out of this dream you two timing piece of shit, you're an unbelievably beautiful fucking dickhead. I don't want to hurt you, but if it means this pain goes away, I will, I reasoned.

"Close your eyes, L.J., and hold out your hand. Then count to five in your head and get ready." He began to laugh to himself. I hated it when he walked away from me laughing, and he knew it. I closed my eyes tightly and imagined my wank bank, bringing into my mind every person I had ever had play time over, so I had a whole army to fight him with me as a backup plan. Behind me stood at least twelve people I'd had serious crushes on, growing up and in adult life. Fancy Pants looked shocked and then started to laugh.

"Jack Nicolson, really?" he fell to the floor crying with laughter. Shit. I'd forgotten about him, I blushed scarlet. "What does he do for you? Open your legs and say 'Heeere's Johnny'?" Tears rolling down his face, he pointed to another person behind me. "Michelle Pfeiffer, mmmm... nice touch I didn't know you were bi-curious? Come over here, baby he offered his hand to her." She walked over to his side and winked at me, blowing me a kiss, and started to lick his face, all dressed up in her cat suit.

"Get off him, bitch!" I screamed out, pissed off that my army was not doing what I had expected it to and feeling insanely jealous and a little turned on.

"Is this person bothering you princess?" I got a smack on the ass and a kiss on lips. It was Danny Dyer, my hero!

"Danny, yes, can you escort this 'dickhead' out of my dream, please? He's been bothering me in my dreams for a while now."

"Can we do that thing again, if I do?" He winked at me wickedly. I smiled back widely, knowing exactly what he was referring to, making Fancy Pants look slightly amused. "Everybody out, come on, it's closing time," he said loudly, squaring up in Fancy Pants' face and staring at him intently.

Then I was in darkness again, holding out my hand waiting for the weapon to be placed in it. A cold object was put in it, it didn't feel like any kind of weapon I could imagine. What had he given me? I counted to five and opened my eyes, we were in darkness again. "Oh, come on, not darkness again. Turn the lights on. I want to kick your fucking ass into next week!" I was jumping up and down on the spot like Rocky getting ready for a fight, when the lights were suddenly turned back on, accompanied by Sinatra's *New York, New York* song blaring out and there he was again, smirking at me, not a care in the world.

"How did you know I was listening to this today?" I rolled my eyes. "Have you been watching me in the shower again? Pervert!"

"I know everything inside your head, you've let me into all your memories and all your feelings; you can't hide or win this fight." He started to do a sexy little dance towards me, stripping off his clothes, and then put his arms behind his back, swinging his dick around to *New York, New York* like he owned the world, enjoying every note of Sinatra. It was a turn on. I had to laugh; he totally owned it. I couldn't stop looking at his amazing penis in front of me, swinging around to the music, and his hairy chest; I was instantly at a disadvantage and massively distracted. He had done this on purpose.

"Put your clothes back on. This is not one of our fucks; this is the end of us," I told his penis, then looked at his face with conviction. He came closer, I could feel his body on mine. He touched my face gently and stroked my hair, getting his fingers caught in my hair extensions and pulled a face. "Look at what's in your hand," he said gently. I reluctantly took my eyes away from his and looked down at my hand. In it was a massive black dildo. "Are you taking the mick?" What the hell? No way I was going to be able to fight with this.

"It's your dream, L.J., not mine." I suppose he was right; my naughty mind had chosen my weapon of destruction. Now I needed to know what he had chosen for his.

"What do you have?" His hand was still behind his back, he smirked in amusement, and then he slowly brought forward what he had in his hand.

"It's the same, only mine is ribbed and pink; I guess these are your choices of preference when you're not with me?" I looked at him in shock that he was right again.

"Well, let's fight then!" I started to walk around him in a circle to intimidate him.

"So, you really want to fight with dildos? I could just slap you with my dick, it's pretty impressive." He looked down at his proud body part and began swinging it around again.

"Don't flatter yourself, it wouldn't do any damage." I grinned and wiggled my little finger up to him in amusement. I put my dildo down on the floor, looked right at him and stripped off all my clothes and threw them at him.

"You've put a few pounds on L.J. Comfort eating?" he looked unimpressed.

That did it, I got mad, really mad, and just glared at him, ready to fight. "Come on then, show me what you're made of!"

He bounced around with his dildo in the air, like it was all some big game to him, making stupid sounds and darting about. I picked up my weapon and hit his dildo a few times, he hit mine and we dropped them on the floor a lot. Then I threw mine at his head and made a run for it.

"You'll never catch me"!" He got up off the floor and looked very amused, rubbing his head. He then started to run after me fast. He chased me around and I dodged him. Finally, he jumped me and pinned me to the ground and then flipped me over to face him. He was on top of me, our naked bodies were touching once more and I wanted him again, even though I hated him so much. He didn't speak, he simply pushed himself inside me and our bodies were back together again.

"I miss you, I miss our fun," I said to him, holding his face with both my hands, looking into his eyes and kissing him hard.

"That's why you had the dream?" He looked at me and kissed me back. Then, with no warning he stuck the massive black cock right up my ass, grinned widely and said, "Until next time, L.J. I win the fight," and he was gone. I sat bolt upright in bed with a yelp, checked my bottom, rolled my eyes and fell back to sleep placing a pillow over my head. God, I'm never going to get over him.

Chapter Two:
The Lady is a Tramp

The smell of strong coffee and diesel filled my nose, making my hangover even worse. Leaning against my new sports car that I couldn't really afford, in my tight pencil skirt, that I found it hard to walk in, wearing heels that I shouldn't legally drive in, I wished I could be back in bed, not having to drive half way across the county to a client meeting. Shades were covering my tired eyes, hiding my wild night of drinking the night before and, as much as I looked like a lady in control, setting about her day, I certainly hadn't been acting like it. My attitude had become worse, my drinking more frequent, as my heart continued to break from Fancy Pants. I had realised that nothing breaks more than the heart, but I was now starting to fight, instead of sitting at home crying over him.

The only way I could cope was to throw myself into my new job, and I was obsessed with writing my book, which took up most of my nights and really entertained me. By writing about what had happened with Fancy Pants, it kept him with me, which was probably completely unhealthy, but writing about him made me feel close to him now that he had completely disappeared from my life. I set off on my journey, smoking out of the car window, blasting out music and not giving a care in the world, wiggling my bottom on the seat to the rhythm, making people passing by me laugh at me and smile. My phone started to ring; it was the office. Pressing the answer button to speaker in my car, I answered brightly.

"Morning, L.J., are you on your way to the meeting, presentation well-rehearsed? Do you have all the handouts?" Knowing how disorganised I could be, he was expecting something to have been forgotten.

"Oh shit, no… I have left them at home!" I smirked in amusement.

"You are kidding me!" he shouted like a cross parent. God, he couldn't take a joke.

"Yeah, I'm kidding! Yes, I've got everything I need, boss. Don't worry about me; I can do this in my sleep! You don't even need to wish me luck," I said with complete conviction.

"Good luck anyway. Oh, and before I forget, please call the company. They have just left a message for you about dinner plans; you're eating out with the director tonight."

"Oh, I am? Okay, thanks for telling me. I take it you've booked a hotel then I've still not had a confirmation email. Somewhere nice I hope?" He always put me in the cheapest, decrepit hotels, anything to save on money, so I was worried what I'd be faced with that night. I suppose anything is better than sleeping in my awful house, at least I get to spend some time away from that dungeon.

Of course, I knew I was eating out with the director. We had planned this quite carefully and we had so much to talk about that wasn't about the presentation. I hung up, lit another cigarette and took a swig of now cold coffee, then speed-dialled the company number. "Good morning it's L.J., for Fox please, I have a message to call about dinner arrangements for tonight," I said, using my best posh Yorkshire businesswoman voice.

"Transferring you now Miss Brown."

I took a deep breath in anticipation of hearing his voice. We had been talking for months over the phone now, some nights until the early hours, him from his hotel rooms around the world, mainly about Fancy Pants, a lot about life and more recently about my book and the hilarious situations I had been getting myself into. I was a mixture of nerves and excitement about meeting him.

"Good morning, young lady..." his deep sexy southern accent was thick with devilment. How can a voice make my stomach lurch and my head light? Perhaps I'm still a little bit drunk from the night before. "How is my favourite writer/consultant today? Are you well prepared for the meeting? HR will be there too and she's very hard to impress, so you will have to knock us both dead to get the business, I'm afraid. No pressure!" He was deadly serious, I could tell.

"Silver Fox, I'm wearing a short pencil skirt and a push up bra, so I'm sure you will be distracted enough to not judge how well I do." I paused, then continued, "Perhaps I should do the presentation on my book; do you think it would go down better?" I smiled from ear to ear, listening to his naughty sexy laugh.

"So, you called about dinner?" he said, quickly changing the subject.

"Yes, I got a message to call you to make arrangements about the dinner I had no idea about," I chuckled. "Our hotels are quite far away from each other I think, where have you booked?" I'd looked at the link I had been sent on my iPhone and had seen that I had been put in some crap B&B, outside of the city centre.

"We are booked into my favourite curry house; the food is beautiful. I take all the ladies there, so they are used to me."

"Is that right. What if I don't like Indian food?" I said coldly, trying to get a reaction.

"Then you can have a salad," he retorted down

the phone.

"Do they have wine?" I had to ask the most important question.

"No, we will have to stop somewhere and pick up a few bottles. Red, I take it from our conversations?"

"Yes," I blushed, he never forgets anything about what I say or do.

"Well, I will get you a taxi, or not drink and take you back to your B&B." I found myself blushing again. He always wanted to make sure I was okay and safe, but all sorts of situations were going through my head. The most worrying one was that I wouldn't be able to control myself, especially after wine, and would sleep with him. "Where are you now? What's your ETA?" he sounded like he had someone near him in the office and the professionalism kicked back in.

"Around two hours. I will be early, so I'm going to get a McDonalds and another coffee before I arrive. I'm hung over to shit. I was deep into writing last night; you know the drill."

There was a long pause, and I could envision him rolling his eyes. "Be safe, young lady. I will see you in the meeting. I'm looking forward to meeting you. Sober up, you need to be on the ball. You won't get another shot at this; we never take meetings from agencies." Then he rang off.

Fuck, he's pissed off with me. I went deep into thought about what to expect from the events of today. I put my foot down on the pedal and overtook a lorry, pressing the sports button I whizzed down the motorway, weaving in and out of traffic. It was a cold March morning and the sun was trying to peep out of the clouds to worsen my hangover. The car was starting to warm up and I felt more relaxed. I'll be with him in a few hours, I thought. I wonder what he looks like, he certainly sounds like a sexy Silver Fox. Perhaps it's all in my head and I'm just over thinking it. He's become a very good friend and friends don't shag, do they? Putting the car into cruise control, I lit up another cigarette and smirked at the fact that I was wearing very expensive matching bra and panties... just in case.

Chapter Three:
Strangers in the Night

Even after lots of stops, I still arrived at the company stupidly early and really in need of a bathroom break, after drinking way too much coffee trying to sober up. I decided to call and see if I could get the meeting brought forward. "Silver Fox, I'm here. I'm ridiculously early. Can you get out of the office for some lunch, or move the meeting? I've got presentation nerves and I need a drink."

"Well, hello again young lady, you did it without getting lost, well done. I can't come to meet you but go to reception and tell them you're here early. They might be able to bring the meeting forward, or at the very least you can grab a coffee and set up your laptop in the meeting room. I'm sorry, I'm in back-to-back meetings. I have to go, see you soon."

"If I drink another coffee, I will turn into one! Not a problem. I will see you soon." I smiled down the phone and we both paused before we hung up. I could tell he was equally as nervous about meeting me, as I was him.

I did as I was told, and HR came promptly to meet me at my car; I didn't even have to go to reception. She was lovely, offering me tea and biscuits and the time to set up for the meeting. I, of course, needed technical help, as I am completely useless with computers, and was directed to the other side of the office, where IT were located. Walking across the office floor back to the meeting room with a member of staff, I saw the Silver Fox for the first time, I recognised him from his LinkedIn photo but he looked very different. Our eyes locked and I smiled widely at him and said hello, but he didn't stop and walked right past me, not saying a word. Confused and bewildered, I thought I had read the messages all wrong and had to shake off the nervous butterflies in my stomach and focus on the task in hand. Right, okay then, you want a presentation. I will give you a fucking presentation, Mr Sexy-doesn't-give-a-fuck. I'm a stupid idiot. Oh my god he's so tall, Silver Fox.

After lots of help, I was ready. HR came in to say the meeting would be on time and to just relax in the room until they arrived. I picked my phone up, texted work to say I had arrived and was set up for the meeting, no hitches. All lies to save my skin. I paced up and down the room with my head down trying to remember the presentation

"Hello, L.J." I jumped, startled; the Silver Fox had slipped into the room silently. He shut the door and apologised for not saying hello, but he was trying to give the impression that he had not talked to, or met me before, only messaged via LinkedIn. I couldn't take my eyes off him. I studied his face. He was a beautiful man, much taller than I had imagined. His eyes were misty blue, and he had big, thick black eyebrows that pointed ever so slightly in the middle, making him look a bit wicked. His hair was thick and silver, and his clean-shaven face was very smooth and manly. He had a serious character. I smiled widely at him and said it was fine, and shook his hand, saying it was nice to meet him.

I don't know if he thought it too, but the first thing that popped into my head was, ''I want to fuck you.' Ashamed, I pulled my hand away and looked down at the floor. I was unable to avoid looking at his crotch; I couldn't help myself. I turned away from him quickly and tried to turn the screen above me on, to start the presentation. I couldn't get it to work and I couldn't look at him again. Oh my god what a disaster and now I had forgotten the presentation and the controls weren't working.

"Let me help," he said softly, and he switched the screen on at the wall. Looking at him, I felt myself glowing redder and redder. He smiled at me, but also looked worried at the same time.

"Thank you," I said, embarrassed. I watched him leave the room and said to myself, "Oh my fucking god who the hell have I just met... what was that?"

I tried to down my tea and missed my mouth, spilling the drink all over myself and the floor. "Fuck, fuck, fuck!" I said under my breath. I had literally forgotten all of the presentation and now was covered in tea. Then they both entered the room talking to each other, ignoring me at first, and shut the door quietly. I stood up, shook their hands and gave the handout to each of them, briefly discussing the presentation, how long it would take and what I aimed to cover.

"Good afternoon, I would like to thank you for inviting me here today, to do this presentation for your company. It should take no longer than twenty minutes and covers everything we discussed originally and how I can help HR going forward with your future business needs." I looked at him sitting there; he was studying the information I had put in front of him, and HR kept looking at me as if to say, "Hurry up, I have things to do."

The presentation was finished in under nine minutes; I read off the cue cards and was so nervous I messed a few words up. I couldn't look at him at any point in the presentation and just looked at the lady from HR like a rabbit in headlights. I had completely messed up. "Any questions?" I hoped they would say, "Nope, you've just messed this up. You can get your coat," and "Who is this loser?" The only thing that could save me was my wet T-shirt under my suit, that might have kept Fox entertained.

"So, do you have any suitable candidates in this industry that haven't moved around much, because that's what we are looking for ideally, people who want to work hard and make this a long-lasting partnership. We don't want job hoppers."

"Yes, of course. I have a few sample CVs. I have taken off the names and companies, but all have worked for direct competitors and, when we get the contract with you, we will have a designated team of head-hunters to do a wider UK search and selection." I felt pleased with myself as HR showed interest in the CV that I had given her.

"*If* you get the contract," the Silver Fox said in a harsh tone, and his face was almost disgusted with my comment. I looked at him, shocked that he had bitten my head off in front of HR. What was he playing at? Why would he do that? The meeting was brought to an end, and they thanked me for my time. I started to pack up. Fuck dinner with this man. What was that all about? What a dick! I had totally messed the meeting up, was absolutely going to get the sack for not closing the contract and now my new trusted friend was fucked off with me for saying the wrong thing. Jesus, I have told him worse things over the phone, and he's been reading my naughty book... How could he? As I was about to leave and make up some excuse to cancel dinner, he came back into the meeting room and closed the door.

I looked at him respectfully and started to speak when he interrupted me "I timed that: 8.5 minutes. I've seen bulls take less time to charge!" His expression was serious, then he smiled and started to laugh "And I'm glad you didn't look at me, you would have completely messed it up then."

"I did mess it up! I knew that presentation off by heart" I flopped down in my seat looking defeated. "Why did you snap at me?" I asked, giving him a bruised glance.

"Oh, come on! I'm not going to make things easy for you. Never assume you've got the business until you're told; it's bad manners. Plus, I had to play a bit of bad cop. I've just told HR I was impressed with the 'content' and that we will do business with you. Now, go grab your coat and meet me in the lobby of my hotel, have a drink and put it on my room tab, I will text you the hotel room number. You can park your car in the hotel car park, and I will get you a taxi to your B&B later, after the meal." He looked at me once more and then left the room, giving me absolutely no chance to object

Driving to his hotel in rush hour took forever, and my phone died in the process. I parked up, left my things in the car and headed to the bar. The hotel was just a basic holiday inn, nothing special, but much better than what my awful B&B would probably be. "Good afternoon, a very large glass of red, please. Merlot if you have it. Please charge it to room two hundred and two, under the name Fox. Oh, and do you have a phone charger please?"

Almost two hours passed before he arrived, and I was well on my way to being a bit tipsy. He would be taking me home tonight for sure, unless things developed. Looking at his penis and messing the presentation up was far from my mind now I had completely relaxed. I had called work and told them I had got the business and was feeling quite smug.

Fox called several times and at last I knew he was not far away. I received a final text letting me know he was in the car park and would only be a few minutes. As he entered the bar, I glanced over and waved to catch his attention and raised my glass asking if he wanted me to get him one. He walked over, very apologetic for being so late, and we walked to the bar to get more drinks. We couldn't stop smiling at each other and he seemed a lot more relaxed and fun now that he was out of work.

"So, the meal, where is it? Do we have far to go? I'm starving!" If I didn't eat soon, I would eat him, but would he quite like that...? I was so unsure.

"Well, I need to freshen up first, don't you? And get changed? Shall I take you to your hotel and pick you up later? We need to nip out for wine too."

"Okay, sure, shall we finish this and get going?"

I wanted him to grab me, to do something to suggest staying with him and get ready in his room, but he didn't make a move and I, after all, even though we were friends, still had to remain professional. We left the hotel and I got my things from my car. We sat in his very posh car in silence for a few minutes trying to figure out where my B & B was for the satnav, when I reached out to grab my bag and we brushed hands. I looked at him, he looked at me and we both blushed and turned away from each other. He then began to talk about his day and how well I'd actually done impressing HR. It was all lies, but I let him talk; he was making me feel special. Then I blurted out, "So, what if I just get ready at yours? My stuff's here already. If you don't mind me using your shower. My B&B is miles away. Let's get the wine and go back to your room." Right then, this made complete logical sense.

"I was going to suggest that actually; it makes sense, right?" He gave me a wicked glance and smiled from ear to ear.

I didn't take my eyes off him for a minute and thought fast. "Yeah, and if something happens between us, then it happens right? I think opportunities like this shouldn't be missed. Do you feel the same way, Silver Fox?" As soon as the words left my mouth, I knew I'd either blown it completely or was going to be having more than a meal tonight. "I mean life's short, right? And I'm not being a tramp; I'm simply saying that you've known me for a few months now. You know I've been through a lot with Fancy Pants and that right now I'm in no man's land, limbo, a place where time stops and anything happens, no strings, no lies. I'm not going to fall in love with you, but we will most probably have reasonable sex tonight, if we ever get that far?" there was a long pause before he replied.

"God, the way you say things in that Yorkshire accent, is so sexy. I agree, but I don't want you to regret anything. I know you've had too much wine already, young lady, so let's see, shall we?"

We messed around in the aisles of the supermarket and bought a few bottles of wine, being silly like teenagers with each other, before finally getting back in the car, with the anticipation of soon being alone in the hotel room together, getting ready to go out.

Once back in the hotel we got into the lift. We looked at each other and the heat between us began to rise, I could feel the pulse between my legs and imagined my lips around his penis. Nothing happened, he was very respectful, and we continued to his hotel room He opened the hotel room door. "It's nothing special, but this is where I spend most of my weeks. It's kind of home to me," he smiled and looked for reassurance.

"It's fine; it's a great room. Shall I shower first?" I looked at him, fiddling with my fingers and my hair nervously. I pulled out leather trousers and heels from my bag and threw them on the bed. "Do you have extra towels?" I pointed to my long hair.

"Sure, the bathroom, it's…" he cleared his throat, "it's just there. Here are some towels." I took them from him and backed away slowly towards the bathroom, watching him, then closed the door. I looked in the mirror. My makeup needed re-applying and I looked tired, but I felt sexy with this man, and confident. Maybe it's because we have been speaking for a few months, that we already know a lot about each other. I was definitely half drunk and I was very horny. Getting ready took me no time at all, and I came out smelling and looking so much better, in my sexy leather trousers and off the shoulder, black top. "Wow," he said, looking at me while I was slipping into my heels, "God, you look amazing!"

"Thank you. Are you jumping in now? Sorry about the mess and make up everywhere. I guess it's okay for me to sleep on the sofa tonight?"

"I will have the sofa and you can have the bed."

Yeah, right, this bed is big enough for both of us, I thought wickedly, no one was sleeping on the sofa unless he screwed up between now and then. He rushed into the shower, so we would figure that one out later. I opened a bottle of the red, filled a cup and started to dance around the room while he was gone. He came back into the bedroom. He scrubbed up very well, his clothes were fashionable, and I was very impressed with his style. With both of us ready to go, he took the wine and, as I was in ridiculously high heels, offered his arm to help me to the restaurant, a short walk from the hotel. We talked about all sorts of things and laughed but got quite drunk. He was talking to me about work and I rested my hands under my chin to listen to him intently. He was very interesting, and I loved his sexy voice. He suddenly stopped talking and looked at me. "You know, I have to be honest, I didn't know what to expect from you, after you telling me about the book and your drinking and crazy behaviour. I wasn't sure if you'd be loud and out-of-control drunk, but you're really quite mellow and very bright." He made a point of telling me not to take it the wrong way.

I kicked my shoe off under the table and brushed my foot up the inside of his leg near his cock, to see if he was feeling what I was thinking. "Do you mean behaviour like this?" I bit into a poppadum and drank some more wine suggestively, thinking it might be sexy, although it probably wasn't.

"Cheque, please," he flagged the waiter and I grinned at him wickedly. "Young lady, every man in this room has looked at you tonight; you don't know your power." He stood up, helped me from my seat and shook the waiter's hand. We both said thank you and staggered out of the restaurant together in the dark, unable to stop smiling and laughing. We both knew what was coming next, just not what order it would unfold.

In the lift we kissed passionately. He had one hand down my panties, playing with my pussy, and the other up my top squeezing my breast hard. We practically ran down the corridor to the room. He opened the door and we were finally alone.

"Put some music on and I'll be back." I escaped into the bathroom to check for food in my teeth and a makeup touch up. Looking in the mirror I felt sexy and ready to get it on with Mr Sexy-Older-Man Silver Fox... Fuck, I hope the Fox has a big tail! "Do you like dancing? Naked dancing? Do you mind if I get naked? I'm drunk, I want to be free." I kissed his neck and started to take my clothes off, scattering them on the floor and dancing around like a hippy, in front of him.

"God, look at you. Wow... Your body is beautiful." He took off his shirt and we kissed, half dancing, half playing with each other, then we were naked, slowly dancing, getting more and more passionate with each other with each beat, kissing each other hard.

I pushed him away. "Watch me," I said, pushing him away further. I danced in front of him, naked, not taking my eyes off him at first, then losing myself in the rhythm and alcohol. I was giving him a private dance, in the middle of his hotel room and he was just sitting there at the end of the bed, not taking his eyes off me. Standing up, he gently pulled me over to him and we fell onto the bed.

He went down on me, wrapping my legs around him so I was locked and couldn't move. He teased me with his tongue and put his fingers deep inside me, taking them out and putting them in his mouth, making me watch while he was tasting me. "Oh my god, stop. I can't take any more. I'm cumming..." I screamed.

"Nope, you're not going anywhere. Cum in my mouth. I want to taste all of you!" He hardly came up for air. I pulled at his hair and screamed again, "Stop! I'm going to squirt." He moved quickly, diving out of the way as my juices gushed out everywhere, onto the bed sheets.

"Oh. My. God," he said in amazement, "that is so sexy. Do it again." And back down between my legs he went; he made me cum five times until I was utterly spent! The bed and the mattress were completely soaked. "I never knew a woman could produce so much. I think I'll have to pay for a new bed." I was so turned on and sensitive I wanted more but was completely exhausted. He went to the bathroom, got some towels, laid them on the bed and positioned his body over mine and I thought he was going to enter me. He slowly picked me up and took me over to our dancing space, and we slow danced and drank more wine. He then picked me up in his strong arms and put me on the desk and, asking me if I was sure with his eyes, entered me slowly.

It was the most intense experience of my life; he was literally worshipping my body. He kissed every part of it and made me feel like I was a goddess in the process. I came over and over. He flipped me and fucked me from behind, banging my head against the wall; we laughed and fell back onto the wet bed. I had been made love to for the first time in my life, but not in any traditional sense, then I turned to kiss him and snuggled into his arms. As he turned out the lights I reached out for a glass of water and poked him in the eye. In hysterics we started to fall asleep in each other's arms like we had never not been there and, for the first time in forever, I felt completely safe. "Well you're a naughty Fox aren't you", I giggled softly into the darkness.

"L J, I don't think there is anyone naughtier than you." He kissed my head and we fell into a deep sleep.

Chapter Four:
I've Got You Under My Skin

I drove home in a daze, re-living the night over and over in my head. I had just seduced a man for whom I had no feelings, no attachment, no intention of anything ever happening other than sex. I have officially become a cold-hearted bitch. Love doesn't live in me anymore; I don't feel, I don't care and I don't want anyone to be any part of me. We had both got exactly what we wanted and needed last night, and I guaranteed I would never see him again. Pulling up to my house, about to enter the dungeon, knowing I was going to be alone all weekend in my own personal hell of a home, I took a deep breath and opened the door. The dusty smell hit me immediately and I opened windows to air the rooms. I walked up the stairs to the bathroom and placed my bag on the landing, pulled out my toiletries and walked into the room to run a hot bath. Sitting on the edge, watching the steam rise, I looked at myself in the long mirror attached to the wall in front of me, that looked as though it was about to fall off.

Who are you L.J? I said to myself and began to cry uncontrollably, what the fuck is going on with you? I no longer recognised myself in the reflection; I was distorted in my head and my mind was in pain. My heart and soul were completely lost in some fragile place that I feared I would never come back from. My phone had died halfway through the journey home, so I had put it on charge in my room. I got into the bath, filled to the top with bubbles. I submerged my body and relaxed, closing my eyes, trying to empty my mind. Flashing through my head were images of kissing the Silver Fox, his eyes looking right into mine, looking into my soul, searching deep inside me for answers he would never find. I could still taste him. How could someone I barely know, understand my body, in one night. How did he light me up more than any man had ever done in my life?

I could hear my phone constantly beeping in the bedroom, so pulling my head under the water to wash my hair, I rinsed the shampoo off my face, reached for a towel that was to hand and wrapped it around my body; my long legs stretching over the bath to get out. Wrapping my hair in a towel, I flopped onto the bed, exhausted from the drive and long night of passionate sex and drinking. I grabbed my phone to check the messages. "Are you home safe, lady?" I had received a message from the Silver Fox, checking that I was okay. I was so surprised. I had expected to be blocked, ignored or given the usual line of 'It was nice to meet you, but I'm just not in the right place, not ready, or still in love with someone else.'

"Hey you. Yes, I'm home safe. I've just had a bath. I really need to sleep; I feel so rough. Are you home safe? You okay?"

"I have images going through my head that I have never had before. God, last night was good, you are so beautiful. So hot! I just wanted to know you were safe." There was a long pause from both of us, in anticipation of what this could be but not knowing really what the hell it was.

"Ah well, you know… it was okay…" I replied with sarcasm and laughed. Smiling from ear to ear, because I knew he got me and wouldn't be offended or become insecure. "You licked my asshole, Silver Fox…" I bit my lip and giggled.

"You cost me a new bed, L.J.," he said seriously. I sat bolted upright in bed, losing my towel.

"I didn't… What, really? They charged you for a new bed!"

"L.J., Noah's Ark would have sunk last night after the amount you produced, plus you broke two cups and a glass. I've never known anything like it, but… it was worth every penny." He smirked over the phone and seemed careless about anything that got in the way of our fun.

"Oh my god, I'm so sorry. I will pay." I felt so embarrassed.

"L.J., it's okay… Please stop worrying about things. I would very much like to see you again, if you want to?" There was another long silence between us while I thought about the situation and how I was feeling.

"I'm a very unusual woman and I'm fucking hard work. No man has ever understood me or tied me down, I'm an enigma. You realise this, yes? This won't be easy for you." I said assertively. I waited for him to get scared and say okay let's just put it down to a great night of wild sex.

"I think I will take my chances, L.J. Let's just see where this goes," he said in a soft reassuring tone. "I don't give many people this amount of time and effort. I've told you before, I don't have feelings; we are in the same place emotionally."

Every time he said this to me it shocked me. His listening skills were above and beyond those of anyone I had ever known. I could tell him literally anything and he would take everything in that I said, soak it in and reflect it back, in the most logical and kind way and would never split hairs, but never talked much about his own feelings and never about love

I grabbed the post that I had thrown on my bed with my phone when I got home and started to open it while talking to him. Pulling out a letter franked from Cambridge, I glanced at it, while listening to him tell me about what he was going to be doing with the rest of the day. "Fuck!" I screamed out in complete shock. I jumped off the bed losing my towel and paced up and down my room.

"What? What is it? Are you okay?" He sounded alarmed. It was usually a gas bill, council tax or some other bill I had not paid in time that got this response.

"I've just got my contract for the book. It's now real!" Jumping up and down on the spot, I said, "Shit, Silver Fox, I've written a pornographic book and it's really going to be published," he laughed and inhaled deeply.

Oh, my Christ, my poor parents! I thought to myself on reflection.

"L.J., my only disappointment, having read the first draft, was that there was not enough; I wanted more." I could feel his delight for me in his tone. "Well done! See, I told you, you could do it."

"I'm an author. I'm really going to have a book published!" I said in complete shock and amazement. I can't even fucking spell, I thought to myself on the bed and laughed loudly, smiling like I hadn't done in years. "I wish you were here right now," I said to him without thinking. I blushed at the thought that I actually really wanted him to be here or someone to share my moment, not an empty house

"L.J., go make yourself some 'cucumber' sandwiches," he said and laughed, knowing I'd be delighted at his comment. I loved his reference to the book but told him I'd had enough cucumber for one night.

Giggling like teenagers again, we were both starting to get tired, having been up so late and driving so far to get home. "I believe in you, L.J. You have a lot of work to do before this book's released, but you can do it. This doesn't happen to many people. Be careful and be safe and get some sleep. I will call you in the morning, if that's okay?"

Pulling myself into bed, I asked him to stay on the phone until I fell asleep. I pulled the covers over me, put my phone on speaker and we talked complete nonsense. Before I knew it, this man was next to me in bed again, in spirit, getting right under my skin, inside my head, stopping me from feeling so lost

. Speaking softly until my words ran out and my dreams began... "Goodnight, sexy fucking Silver Fox..."

"Goodnight, my crazy little squirter author."

Chapter Five:
Old Devil Moon

Shooting upright in bed, I rub my eyes, yawn and sit on the side of my bed, reaching for my glasses. I stumble to the bathroom to get dressed. Dancing and singing in the shower, was now my everyday routine; it was a ritual to make sure I stayed positive and happy in my miserable lonely existence. Washing my hair, I got an awful feeling of being watched. This had happened a few times since I moved into the dungeon; it made the hair on my neck stand up and, even though hot water was running all over my body, I suddenly felt freezing. My heart pounding in my ears, I pulled the shower curtain back and looked all around the room, but no one was there. I stepped out of the shower, closed the door and locked it. "If you're dead, you're stiff already. Fuck off! Perving at me..." I choked out into thin air. The house I rented not only smelt of shit and dog, I was now 100% sure that Kim Woodburn and Yvette Fielding would have a field day busting grime and ghosts.

Having quickly dressed, I ran down stairs and set the kettle to boil for a much-needed cup of Yorkshire tea and waited for my phone to power up. I was dreading millions of work emails to catch up on and wondering if the Silver Fox would have slept on it and decided to end things, after I'd cost him a new hotel bed.

Good morning, young lady. You okay? I smiled from ear to ear that he was still thinking of me.

Silver Fox, I'm finding it hard to sit down. I sent the text and gave out a silly giggle, then waited for his response.

The phone immediately rang. "Mmmm, I keep having flashbacks, you were amazing." I blushed, he has really been thinking about me, but I was still unsure how I felt, I tried not to seem desperate or needy.

"I can still smell you on my clothes." I smiled, picking up my washing basket and being overwhelmed by the smell of his aftershave on my top, giving me a slight crunch in the pit of my stomach.

"I can still taste your pussy," he said with devilment in his deep, hungry voice. I dropped the washing basket and paid him my full attention. I heard a deep sigh. "I love your sexy Yorkshire accent, and that body... I can feel the heat of your pussy wrapped around my cock."

I bit my lip and crossed my legs. "I had a dream about you last night," I whispered… "I'll tell you about it next time I see you."

"Was I naked?" he asked and chuckled.

"No, but I was," I smirked and knew, even over the phone, he was struggling to control himself.

"So, you're officially going to be an author. Has the shock hit you yet?"

I was surprised at the change of subject but delighted to talk about it. "I have to put my journal together now and make it make sense. Yes, I'm excited, but a little scared. I sent it as a joke, I never expected in a million years I would be accepted by a publisher. Silver Fox, every time I wrote about what was happening to me, I was pissed." I gave a deep sigh and started to worry about how much hard work I had let myself in for.

"Believe in yourself, L.J.; you're perfectly capable of doing anything in life. If you don't try, you will never know," he said in a supportive tone. "Just keep your head screwed on." He was always so full of great advice and knew just how to calm me down.

"Have you eaten? Did you sleep well?" I loved the way he always worried about me, not many men I'd dated ever had. Listening to me completely fall apart over the last few months when we were still only friends, had put him in the habit of being concerned for my welfare. I had lost a few stone through not caring if I lived or died. I had forgotten that he had listened to my heartbreak and that if I hadn't had the Silver Fox at the end of the phone, I'm not sure I'd still be alive to tell this tale.

"Yes, I had some toast and I'm going food shopping today, and, yes, I did sleep. You had kept me up all night... so I needed it." I smiled down the phone and touched my lips with my finger.

"So, no kids all weekend. What are your plans?" He sounded satisfied with my answer and moved on from the lecture.

"I'm going to write the fuck out of the weekend," I shouted out jumping up and down on the spot, spilling my tea.

"You go, girl. I hope you get lots done and enjoy yourself. Don't forget to buy a cucumber," he giggled.

"Come over here and I'll stick it up your ass," I playfully suggested, hoping he would at least mention another possible meeting.

"You're not sticking anything up my ass, but I certainly will be sticking something up yours," he said with a smoky voice.

"I need to arrange some interviews with you, so can we call another meeting? I'll come to you this time," he changed the subject, suddenly sounding professional.

"Yes, just let me know and I will arrange it. When were you thinking?" I powered up my laptop to check my calendar.

"Next week at your office. I'd like to meet your MD and we can go through the CVs. I will tell him how good you are at your job; you need a pay rise. I have a few ideas for your company and a lot of contacts to pass on to you, also some suggestions for a few shows and exhibitions you should attend."

"So, you've just had your head in between my legs and now you want to sit across a desk from me and talk business? You will get a hardon in the office," I joked with him, hoping he wasn't serious.

"Twenty-second at three p.m. Get a babysitter and I will take you out for dinner. I will send you the agenda."

"Okay, it's pencilled in, you bossy fucker. Oh shit, that's next week," I said, surprised.

"Yes, it is… I look forward to seeing you again. I will call you tomorrow, I have to go to football now. Have fun writing and take care young lady." He hung up and I stared into space then danced around my tiny kitchen and up the narrow steps shaking the moves like Jagger, getting myself organised for the dreaded budget food shop.

Rushing around the supermarket as instructed, passing the vegetable aisle and grinning widely to myself, I grab a bottle of wine and dash to the busy check out. Checking my phone for messages, I went to my WhatsApp and hovered over Fancy Pants to tell him the good news about the book. Then thoughts about the Silver Fox filled my head and unexpected guilt overcame me. I stared into space for a few minutes and then went back to my phone and deleted his number. After the last time I saw him and what had happened, he didn't really deserve my time. Why should I tell him anything, even if he had asked me to let him know? After driving home and unpacking, I ran a bubble bath and poured myself a glass of wine, taking my journal into the bath with me, to read my notes and refresh my mind. I had given the publisher three sample chapters and a preface. They were random, all over the place, because I didn't have things tied together yet, no plan of how to tell the full story. Where should I start? I had written so much. Flicking through, I started to re-live the pain, the passion, the drama and the fun of the previous twelve months. I should be at least twenty stone from eating all that tiramisu and drinking so much wine, I thought to myself.

"What a fucking bastard," I shouted out, throwing the journal on the floor and sinking into the bath with my glass of wine. Knowing how much pain he had caused me, how much he had used me, was one thing, reading about it in my notes and remembering crying myself to sleep while writing in my journal, because I'd been blocked and couldn't tell him by text, was quite another. It had had to come out somehow, I had been slowly going mad with his rejection and I was reading about how I had fallen for it every time.

The wine had gone to my head, so I made myself some food and sat down to the table with my laptop, ready to write. Turning the music up, my fingers tapped the keyboard at a hundred miles an hour, revisiting every memory, pouring out emotions I needed to deal with. I laughed at the fun bits and sobbed deeply, feeling the heartache. Taking off my clothes, dancing around to the music, wine in one hand, pencil in the other, like a conductor at my own orchestra, I closed my eyes and my mind went back to the last time I had seen Fancy Pants.

"Oh wow, they look amazing on you," my sister said, looking at me wearing tight leather trousers in the changing room., "You have to get them," she was impressed and looked lovingly at me.

"You don't think I'm too old for leather trousers, do you? Does my bum look fat?" I'd lost confidence and was trying to buy things to make me feel happy. I never ate to cover my feelings, I drank and bought clothes.

"Do it!" She looked at the price tag and said, "My treat." I insisted on getting them myself, but she just wouldn't give in. She had worried over me more than usual recently, like everyone else, trying to be a parent more than a sister.

"Shall we grab a quick coffee with lots of chocolate sprinkles? My treat as a thank you." I grabbed her hand and dragged her into the nearest coffee shop. We sat down and as I warmed my hands around the cup, we both checked our phones. I looked up at her, my face expressionless.

"What is it L.J?" she looked at me, concerned.

"It's him. He's asked how I am. I've not heard from him for months; I deleted his number earlier today. I can't believe this. What do I do?" I looked at her, completely perplexed.

"Don't reply; he's a complete tosser. Lose this person L.J!" She took my phone off me and looked at the message, shaking her head.

"He's got some guts; I'll give him that. I hate this man; he's not good for you. Please ignore him."

I slipped my phone into my pocket and we drank in silence. We didn't need to talk about him. We had covered this subject many times from every angle and the answer was always the same; he was never going to change.

"What about that guy you've been talking to? He seems really nice, so why don't you try to go on a date with him?"

"He's just a friend and a client. I can't get involved with him, plus he's older than me and has an amazing life. He wouldn't want a poor single mum with no prospects. He's not shown me any attention, sis, he just finds me interesting and we have work in common. I'm hoping to find him a lot of staff, plus we haven't even met yet". I inhaled deeply and took my phone back out of my pocket reading the message from him over and over. We finished our coffees, hugged each other tightly and went our separate ways. Shouting across the car park, "Don't reply!" she instructed me assertively and was gone.

Walking through town back to my house, I read the message and decided not to text back. Instead I bit my lip. My heart pounding in my chest uncontrollably, I pressed the call button, with no idea what I was going to say.

"What do you want?" he answered playfully.

"You texted me," I giggled, and my real smile came back to life, after being dead for months. It was so good to hear his voice.

"I didn't think I would hear from you again, after what you said to me in the car."

He ignored my comment. "What are your plans today?" he asked, direct as usual.

"I've just been shopping for new clothes. I'm going out tonight for dinner with a friend, not far from you actually," I said brightly.

"Well, I'm free tonight. I thought that we could perhaps talk, but if you're busy..." He started to become distant and we both took a long pause trying to work each other out.

"The meal's at seven p.m. I can come up around nine-ish?" I knew we needed to do this; I was just scared of the time apart and the fact that I might have sex with him again and get thrown to the wolves.

"*Bon appétit*, I will see you then." And he ended the call, leaving me feeling sick with nerves, but floating above the floor at the same time; my smile warmed everyone that passed me by in the street.

Over the meal with Emma, I couldn't stop talking about him and what might happen. I covered every possible situation and even the chance of him cancelling, until he texted halfway through the meal to tell me not to get wine, that he'd already bought some.

"I'm due on, Emma what happens if he wants to have sex?" I blushed and looked worried, stuffing my face with steak.

"You will have sex L.J.; you know you will."

I shrugged my shoulders, because I really didn't know this time. "He said he wants to talk. We both know what he said when I was in the mountains, months ago. Is he opening up to me?" I looked to her for reassurance.

"L.J., he's not going to talk to you. He will tell you anything to get you back into bed. That is all he wants from you. I've warned you, but you just won't listen." She called for the waiter to get the bill and we gathered our things to leave. Pulling up outside his house, the lights were on, so I called him from the car to say I had arrived, and he promptly opened the door. I got out of the car, taking a deep breath.

"Hi," was all I could say, staring into his eyes, looking at him and searching for answers as to why he'd asked me there. He was so fucking perfect to me, the way he looked, the way he smelt. I couldn't take my eyes off him. All I wanted to do was run across the room and kiss him, but I couldn't. I couldn't make myself go near him I was so hurt.

"Nice trousers," he observed, "And flat shoes. Not like you." He smiled, showing his perfect white teeth.

"Well, you know, you're a short ass. I thought I'd help you out a bit," I grinned at him, still full of nerves and very aware I was completely sober.

"Your hair. It has grown back," he winked in amusement.

"It's clip in. I still have hair like Worzel Gummidge." I told him the truth; the bloody thing would probably fall out if we shagged anyway. He grimaced and walked across to the fridge.

"Glass of wine?" he asked, to change the subject.

"Yes please." I needed a drink so badly, to steady my nerves. He poured the drinks and we got close to each other. As usual, I jumped up onto his work top, fully dressed for a change and he leaned against it next to me. Our eyes locked and I swigged the wine down, handing it back to him for a refill, he rolled his eyes and topped me back up.

"You look sad, what is it?" I asked, when he handed me the wine.

"I just have a lot going on." He looked at me; his eyes searching for answers I couldn't give him. Oh shit, there really was something wrong. Had he been drinking? Was he dying? Was he about to tell me it was over forever?

"Talk to me," I said softly.

"My son's decided not to continue with school but start work; things have just been very difficult with trying to help him make the right decisions." He talked to me for what seemed forever, about school and work and his family. He told me how many brothers and sisters he had (although he didn't want to talk about his brother for long). He told me his children's names and spoke about his mother. I was in complete shock that this man who had hidden away and been so private about everything for so long, now was suddenly opening up his world to me.

"Everything will be okay. You're doing a good job; being a parent is hard," I took his hand and kissed it without thinking.

"Are you seeing anyone L.J?" He looked at me, still holding my hand.

"No, I'm finding the path of love very difficult. I can get a date, or even a shag, anytime I want, but nothing's been enough. No one has filled that empty space. Do you know what I mean?"

"It's about connection," he said, welling up with tears and fighting them back.

"It's hard to find, isn't it?" I looked at him, searching for answers and thinking to myself, please just say it, say we have it.

I jumped down off the kitchen top and leaned into him, looking into his eyes, loosening his belt and undoing his top button. I put my hands down his pants and grabbed his rock-hard cock. "Connection," I said, leaning in to kiss him. He grabbed the back of my head but quickly let go realising that my hair really was clip in and we both laughed.

Moving into the front room, I noticed that he had lit candles all around the room. I looked at him in amazement. "Romance?" I teased him sweetly and gave him an unbelievably grateful smile.

"L.J., you've been in my house nearly an hour and are still fully dressed." He smirked at me and I pushed him down on the sofa. Standing across the room, I stripped off to the music on the TV, twirling my clothes around my head and then throwing them at him, hitting the light fixture.

"Don't break my house again," he complained. I climbed on top of him, sat down and started to slowly pull his pants down, but had not thought about the logistics of this and struggled. Finally, off they came and my favourite cock in the world was there to play with again. Both our eyes lit up in excitement.

"Discover a new kind of freedom: tampon freedom. Why compromise?" An advert had come on between songs and we both started to laugh. "It's not only more discreet, but it's plastic applicator makes it even easier to use," it continued.

"Oh my god, now it's just killing the mood. When are you going to get yourself a play list?" It didn't help that I was actually due to come on and it could literally happen at any time. How ironic.

"Shall we have a fag?" he said, throwing back his wine. I looked confused and got off him.

"Sure, if you're okay with me standing outside naked." I twirled around and did a silly little dance in front of him.

"Here, wear my coat," he pointed to the pile of coats and reached into a cupboard for his cigarettes.

"It's a bit small." I turned to him, struggling to wear the coat and looking puzzled.

"That's because it's my son's; that one's mine."
He gave me a 'you're so stupid sometimes' look and
walked out with me into the garden.

The coat barely covered half of my ass, so I was
still almost naked. I walked out into the garden and
bent over, teasing him and came back to him
bouncing around like Tigger in the cold, trying to
keep warm.

"Listen, I have something to tell you. I had been
waiting for the right moment." I wasn't even sure I
was going to tell him. "I'm writing a book, I've just
been signed with Pegasus, about my experience of
being single after leaving my marriage, I hope you
don't mind, but you are in it. I've not mentioned your
name in the book obviously; you're called Mr Fancy
Pants. Looks like it could really take off."

"A book? Really?" He started to laugh... "I
could be looking at the next J.K. Rowling? Well,
people had to read it, to sell so..., but good for you;
I'm impressed. I have never met a writer before."
Throwing his cigarette on the floor, he waited for me
to finish mine.

"I'm really excited, but I have a lot of work to do
on it. Would you like me to send you some to read?"
Excitedly, I looked at him.

"I want to get warm," he looked at me waiting to
get me back inside. I was pretty sure he didn't believe
that I was writing a book.

Coming in from the cold, I dropped his coat. He took my hand we walked through the hallway, up the stairs and he threw me on the bed, pushing himself inside me immediately. I'd missed him so much.

"God, I love your pussy," he said, struggling to talk, looking at me and waiting for a response.

"Maybe your cock and my pussy should get married then?" What the fuck did I just say, oh my god, do I literally have no filter? I blushed and then screamed out with pleasure, trying to save the moment. He lifted my legs and placed himself inside my bottom, throwing his head back in absolute pleasure, looking at me and biting his lip. I twisted and moaned. He did it for a lot longer than usual.

"Fuck!" he shouted out, looking at me in complete shock that he had just made me squirt while fucking my ass.

"How is that even possible?" I yelped, looking at him as shocked and overwhelmed as he was. He left to wash, came back and we made love, holding each other so tight and kissing like we would never let go, until we were completely spent. Collapsing on the bed next to me, he pulled my head to his so our foreheads were touching. Neither of us could move from the level of intensity and mental connection we had just experienced together; we were absolutely exhausted. I had never been so tired after sex.

Holding each other close, we talked for a bit and then began to fall asleep in each other's arms.

"I love you," I said softly. He didn't say it back; he pretended to be asleep. I watched him sleeping for a long time, thinking about what had just happened and how it had felt. Once I was sure he was completely asleep, I got up, dressed and kissed him goodbye. That old devil moon in his eyes, I'd fallen for it again; he didn't love me and he never would, I wish I'd listened to my sister and not gone, I felt worse now than ever before

All that time had passed and now I had written about it, our very last time. Emailing two of my friends a few more chapters to edit for me, I closed my laptop down, took my last swig of wine, dragged myself up the stairs, threw myself on the bed and cried myself to sleep, thinking to myself that I hoped I never see that awful man again

Chapter Six:
Have Yourself a Merry Little Christmas

Having been sent home from work, I called the doctor and he sent me straight to hospital for an x-ray. It was such a bad time for things to be going wrong. I had a client meeting that I needed to attend with the Silver Fox and had to rearrange because of illness. "You have pneumonia, Miss Brown. You will continue to feel confusion and disorientation for a few days; the dizziness, coughing and fever are all symptoms. I'm afraid you are going to have to stay in hospital." The doctor gave me a thoughtful look and checked my pulse again.

"But it's Christmas Eve. 'Can't you give me some antibiotics and send me home? My kids' Christmas will be ruined."

"I'm afraid that, because you are coughing up blood, you need to stay here for a few days," he looked down through his glasses at me, as if I was a naughty child.

"Have you been out in the cold for long periods of time, or near any damp?" he questioned me, to find out how I'd got into this awful state. I thought for a moment and then realised that the dungeon I'd been living in was probably the root cause of the illness.

"My house is damp. I sleep next to a wall and window covered in mould. I've not been able to afford to move out and the landlord won't do anything to help." I looked at him embarrassed and ashamed at my situation but too tired to try to lie or make up an excuse.

"Well, I suggest it's time to call on friends and family, to help you get out of this situation, or perhaps environmental health. You need to find new accommodation and start looking after yourself." He picked up the clipboard, filled out some information and placed it at the bottom of the bed. "Merry Christmas, Miss Brown. Try to get some rest, and you will be out of here by Boxing Day, I'm sure." With a reassuring smile, he turned and left.

For fuck's sake, I'm going to have to text my ex and ask him to keep the kids over Christmas. I tried to text, but the drip in my hand still hurt me. I could barely find the energy to see what I was writing. *'Hey, I'm still in hospital. It's more serious than I thought. I'm afraid I'm going to be stuck here for Christmas, so you will have to keep hold of the little monkeys. I'm sorry if it spoils your plans, can't be helped. Please don't spoil Christmas by letting them see me like this, keep them away.'* I sent the text and then started to cough, bringing up blood, I pressed the buzzer and a nurse came. "It's time to take some more meds, Miss Brown, you will find yourself quite sleepy. Can I get you anything else while I'm here?" I had the most awful nurse; she was so uncaring and brash. 'What's happened to the NHS? It's fucking Christmas, I should be getting a Christmas carol and a box of chocolates.

"Thank you, I'm fine." Hiding my phone under the pillow, I saw a reply, a thumbs up, and I rolled my eyes. He's pissed off and doesn't even care. I sent one more text before my eyes started to get heavy, to Mr Fancy Pants telling him what had happened; he read it and didn't reply. Tears rolling down my face, I looked up at the hospital ceiling and said to myself, "Merry fucking Christmas L.J.," and I was asleep. I drifted so far away that the noise around me became a distant echo, deeper and deeper into the darkness. I couldn't feel my body anymore; I was floating; it was soothing and peaceful like floating on water. Finally, I was having a rest from everything. I'd needed this; I needed to heal.

"L.J. Brown!" A voice bellowed at me from nowhere. I shot upright and looked all around me.

"Who is it?" I questioned, not recognising the voice, but not scared of it. I looked behind and all around and my body was lying on the floor. "Oh fuck, I look like shit... I hope no one sees me." Then I looked at myself again. "Fuck, oh holy fuck, am I dead?" I turned around searching for answers, not able to see any light anywhere, although I could see shadows. "Am I in hell? Where's the light…? I'm supposed to go to the beautiful light and all that crap, right?" I shrugged my shoulders and started to get cross at getting no reply.

"Where the fuck am I?" I shouted loudly and stomped my feet. "I'm not well, you know. I'm supposed to be resting and it's Christmas. Don't you have to go celebrate your birthday or something? FYI, I don't believe in you, so you can just go away!" I fell to the floor coughing and slumped next to my body, the only thing I could see properly. I looked so thin, so pale and so very ill, maybe I was dead.

"You are not in hell, or heaven. We don't know what to do with you, actually; you are an odd split of good and bad that we have never seen before. Your sexual habits are out of control and we do not agree with your language, but your heart seems to be kind and vulnerable… We've never had anyone quite like you before."

"I don't need help; I'm fine. There are plenty more people in much worse situations that actually believe in God so just go." I said angrily, remembering a time when I used to think he was real and the bird on my windscreen.

"You think you have a bad life?" the voice questioned me further.

"Yes, I hate it. 'It's awful. No one wants me, no one likes me, and I have nothing." I started to cry. "I'm sick. 'Can't you just heal me and then you've done your bit?"

"You have to heal yourself, but we have given you everything. You have two beautiful children and we saved you from the car accident. Be kind to yourself and respect yourself always." I looked up and there was light shining into my eyes. It was so bright I couldn't look directly at it and had to cover my eyes, then once again I was thrown into darkness. "Well, well, well, if it's not L.J. Brown." It was a deeper more mysterious voice this time; the room was freezing cold and I felt uncomfortable and in danger.

"Don't listen to him; it's his birthday and he's been on the wine. I sympathise; your life is really shit isn't it! But hey... I'm your biggest fan. I can't wait to get Fancy Pants down here; he's going to cause quite a stir with the ladies." I paused and thought about Fancy Pants being in hell and flirting with all the deviant women. I guess he would love it. I was instantly on the defensive.

"He's Catholic actually, I think he'll be in the penthouse upstairs," I disagreed with him, instantly wanting to protect him from his fate, then trying to

71

change the subject. "You like my writing… what is your favourite bit?" I joked with him, smirking at some appreciation.

"My favourite bit, you've not written yet, so unfortunately you must go back. I'd love to stay and party with you L.J., but you have more corruption to do for me." He chuckled loudly. "I love the tree chapter; I did laugh. I was watching you for hours. I want to torture you L.J., and if you carry on the way you are going, I will get you down here and you will be one of my favourite toys." I froze to the spot. I had felt the evil. I was then struck by something hard in my chest. It felt like fire and I couldn't move for pain.

"What are you doing to me?" I screamed out and then felt another surge to the chest, like electricity was flowing through my body. "Are you possessing me, because it won't work. I've seen The Exorcist; I will get a priest to stick a crucifix right up your…"

BEEEP…

"Stand back. One, two, three." I heard a voice close to my face and I could feel someone touching me. There was a long silence. "She's back. Good work team." I recognised a doctor's voice. There was a cheer and I could hear people clapping. Then I dozed into a deep dreamless sleep.

Chapter Seven:
Fly Me to the Moon

It had been weeks since my near-death experience and arguing with God. I'd had to take some time out to rest and reorganise life; top of my list was moving out of the dungeon. The shock of me being ill and the house being unsafe for habitation had quickly persuaded my parents to support me financially to move and I had found a nice new house which was near my job I was packing boxes again feeling happy about moving my life and the children's schools, hopefully for the last time. My first day back at work was a tell-tail sign that they were not impressed with me being off for so long and this wasn't going to be my forever job, but I put my head down and got on with it. I couldn't argue with the person that put food on my table.

"L.J., line two. It's Fox about the meeting." One of the office assistants announced the call to me, before putting it through.

"Good morning, L.J. speaking." I pulled up my calendar on my computer. I knew he was coming to the office this afternoon for a meeting. I'd not seen him since the hotel room, and over Christmas he'd been busy with his children, so I had not heard much and didn't want to tell him how ill I had been.

"Hello L.J., did you have a nice Christmas? Are you prepared for the meeting today? I just wanted to check it was still on, as I have an appointment just before, so I might run slightly late."

I could feel myself blushing at his sexy voice, it still had the ability to turn me on. "Yes, I'm fully prepared. Are we still going out for dinner afterwards? My manager can't make it, so it's just going to be us." I grinned down the phone, because I was glad that I'd have him all to myself for a while.

"What are you wearing L.J? If I was there right now, I'd have you over your desk, with my head buried between your legs, ready to fuck you senseless."

I paused and crossed my legs. Whispering into the phone "I'm not wearing any panties," I grinned and then changed the subject. "So, we are covering sales staff?" I tried to be as informative as possible with my conversation, not really caring about the meeting, more about the meal and possible hotel room afterwards.

"I will cover you, everywhere. I'm going to put my rock-hard cock deep inside you, until you cum harder than you ever have before, and then I'm going to do it all over again. God, I can feel myself inside you L.J." My heart sank in between my legs and I began to feel my pulse rate rise. The lust waves had begun and all I wanted to do was grab him by his penis, drag him into the meeting room and ravish him.

"So, what do you like to drink, tea or coffee?" I tried to bring back control, with everyone in the office now looking at my flushed face.

"I'd prefer to drink you, but coffee one sugar will do fine. I'll see you in a few hours L.J. Oh, and make sure you sit near me, so I can play with you under the desk, if you're not wearing any panties." Unable to answer him back, I hung up.

"Fox okay and still on for the meeting L.J?" my boss shouted across the office, looking worried.

"Yes." I cleared my throat. "All okay. He's got a lot to talk about, so just be warned, we might be in there for some time." I looked across at him confidently.

"Well, I'm handing the meeting over to you L.J. I want you to do all the hard work; I will just take a few notes. Seems like you have everything under control." I put a thumbs up to him and smiled; little did he know what would be going on under the table.

I returned from my lunch and went to the bathroom to freshen up before he arrived, cleaning my teeth and spraying myself with perfume. A few make up touches and I appeared to look okay. I was wearing a smart black short work dress with a jacket and heels. I'd had a spray tan and my hair extensions were in a reasonable state, but above all I felt confident and sexy and I was really looking forward to seeing him again.

"L.J., it's for you, a candidate enquiry." I dashed across the office to my desk and picked up the call. As soon as I answered the phone, the Silver Fox arrived. Stuck on the phone, I couldn't greet him, so I gestured to my boss, who got up, rolled his eyes and took him into the meeting room. Fox looked at me, I looked at him and I felt like someone had winded me; my heart started to pound, and my legs were weak. I started to play with my hair, and I put my face down to avoid eye contact, ending the call as quickly as possible, so I could go to be with him.

Getting tangled up in the phone wire and almost tripping over a folder, I escaped from my desk and dashed to the meeting room. "Fox, it's wonderful to meet you again. Did you have a pleasant journey?" He got up and we shook hands before sitting down opposite each other. I had to make sure I wasn't too close; I knew his intentions. He looked at me in amazement, his eyes wide, his posture open, and we both blushed a little. "As I discussed with you in our last meeting, we are passionate about moving the business forward. We invited you here today to discuss ideas; as we know you are well networked in the industry." I rushed my words, thinking about the hotel bed I had broken and the naked dancing.

The Silver Fox reached for some water, and a pen and paper and began to draw a diagram for us. He turned to my boss. "I have to say, I get contacted by a lot of recruiters, but this young lady has done your company proud. We have not needed to use an agency for years, as our reputation is second to none; people come to us. But she has a talent. You must feel lucky to have her on board." He smiled at me, then he looked at my boss for a reaction.

"She's a good one. We are very proud of her, although she's not been here long." He winked at me.

Well, give me a bloody pay rise then, you tight bastard, I thought to myself, right after feeling the respect that had come from the very sexy Silver (Oh my god yes, you are going to get laid today) Fox!

The meeting lasted around an hour; we went through ideas and came up with an action plan. Several roles were discussed and so I had officially won a major contract and was very much in the good books.

"L.J., I will leave you to finish the meeting. I have to dash; kids parents evening, sorry. It was fantastic to meet you. I will leave you in L.J.'s capable hands." They shook hands and then my boss was gone, as was everyone else in the office, apart from one consultant. The door was shut, and we were alone.

"Oh my god, Fox, thank you so much. That was great; what an amazing meeting. I promise I will find you a top dog sales manager." I smiled at him and reached for his hand to hold it. We looked at each other for what seemed forever, and then I kicked off my heel and brushed my foot across the inside of his leg, like I did in the restaurant that first time.

"Let's get out of here," he said wickedly. We slowly got out of our seats, gathered our things and, acting like professionals, left the building. "You can leave your car here; I will bring you back to work later on today. Let me take you to dinner in style." He flashed his posh car at me; I giggled and got in. We sat looking at each other and desperately wanted to kiss.

"Not here, let's drive off. We don't want to be seen; I will get the sack," I said in desperation, not wanting to be found out.

"God, you are beautiful." He looked at me, touching my face, and then turned away to start the engine. We travelled out of the centre of town, on to a country road, heading to the hotel where he was staying, and we were having dinner.

I grabbed his hand and guided it between my legs, so he could feel that I wasn't wearing any panties. Before I knew what was happening, he had his fingers deep inside me, making me go wild with pleasure. We didn't talk we just looked at each other. He pulled his fingers out of me, then put them in his mouth and licked them clean, making sure I watched him, then put his finger in my mouth.

"Hotel room before dinner?" I suggested to him. I wanted to have sex so badly, I thought I was going to burst.

"No, I think we should go for a quick drink. I want to take you out and kiss you in front of everyone." He had that devil look in his eyes again; I loved how much he wanted me.

We arrived at a country pub and pulled in. We walked into the bar and ordered drinks, then sat out of the way, where we could have some privacy. As soon as we were seated, our lips locked and we couldn't stop kissing, like teenagers; it was wild and passionate and addictive.

"I want to fuck you, Fox," I whispered into his ear. He looked at me and told me I looked drunk. "I've had half a glass of wine; I must be drunk on you," I replied.

A dog bounced its way towards us, knocking our drinks over. The Fox grabbed the dog and began to be playful with it, telling it that it was okay and it was just a drink. Babies and now animals. Could this man be any nicer? I thought to myself. I started to mop the mess up with my jacket and he told me off. We moved tables, had one more drink and several more kisses, and left to go to the hotel.

We pulled up outside the hotel, checked in and held hands to the hotel room, looking at each other and not saying much until we got to the door. He put the card in, we went inside and instantly turned into animals, ripping each other's clothes off and kissing each other like our lives depended on it. We banged into walls, we fell over things and finally landed on the bed, so desperate to be inside each other, we didn't even bother with foreplay.

"Fuck, L.J., you feel so good." He pounded into me slowly and pinned me down to the bed, kissing me hard, biting my lip and neck and nipples.

"Fox," I shouted out breathless, "Oh my god, Fox, I'm cumming…!" As I screamed out his name, he covered my mouth. Holding me down, biting my lips, letting me scream into his mouth, over and over again and again, as he looked deep into my eyes.

"Again, L.J., I want you to cum again." He turned me around, so I was on top of him, rubbing my clit up and down with him deep inside me, and I started to build. "I want to see your face as you fall apart." He locked my legs under him and pushed me back and forth slowly, the energy inside me built, making me shake and eventually I exploded and screamed out in complete pleasure. He pulled me off his cock and quickly up onto his face and drank me, licking my clit that was already so sensitive. He made me cum again and again into his mouth, and he loved it. Exhausted, we both laid down on our backs on the bed out of breath and then turned toward each other and kissed passionately. "Let's go get a shower L.J. and then have dinner." He kissed my forehead and pulled me up, looking at my body and worshipping it with his eyes.

He started the shower and we got in together, kissing and soaping each other up. He stuck the soap inside me; I was shocked and stopped him. "What are you doing?" I asked, "'That's not good for a lady; I'll get sore!" I blushed.

"Oh, I am sorry." He then tried to stick it in my ass and we both laughed out loud. Turning me around he entered me slowly from behind and I heard him moan. It was now his turn. "I wish you could see what I'm seeing right now; what an amazing sight the water is, bouncing off your bottom. It's kind of beautiful... your body..."

"I want you to put your cock in it. Would you like to try?" I whispered in a sexy husky, worn out voice. He rubbed soap on me. There was a long silence and then he was entering me slowly. It pinched and burned and then it felt good. I didn't want to ask, but I imagined it to be his first time.

"L.J., this is, well... oh fuck... I'm going to cum..." He was ruined.

"Cum. I want you to cum hard for me, Fox." He pulled out, , then entered me and fucked me harder than I've ever known. My hands pushed up against the shower wall, I could hardly see for steam all around me. All I could hear was both of us moaning and time disappeared, while I was having the most intense orgasm of my life. With the shower still running we collapsed in the bath and kissed, my makeup was all over my face and coming off into the bath but I didn't care He held my face and kissed me everywhere; every part of me.

Grabbing towels, he wrapped me up and we snuggled and kissed, then started to get dressed. Talking about the day and laughing about everything, we were just like best friends again. Best friends that wanted to fuck all the time. Then came the noise, I crossed my legs and ran to the bathroom. Fuck, I thought to myself, don't let this mess everything up.

"L.J., what's wrong?" There was a knock at the bathroom door, but I quickly locked it.

"It's fine. I will be out in a minute." I sat on the toilet and turned the tap on, so he couldn't hear. What the fuck? With the all the fanny farts, my lady bits were literally growling like an animal. "Shut up, fucking stop it, now!" I looked down and pointed in anger.

"Are you being sick, L.J?" the Fox shouted through the door.

I tried to think fast. "No, honestly, I'll be okay in a few minutes. I promise."

"Okay. Are you sure you don't need me L.J?" He sounded concerned.

"Oh, Fox, I don't know what to do," I shouted back.

"What? What is it?" He sounded genuine enough to listen to what was wrong, so I decided to explain.

"We have a growler!" I unlocked the bathroom door. He walked in and we both burst into laughter at me standing there with my hand around my lady bits trying to stop them from making unpleasant sounds

"I'll order room service L.J." He looked at me sympathetically and he kissed my forehead. This guy's irreplaceable.

Chapter Eight:
Ring-a-Ding-Ding

"Come on children, out of the door, as quick as you can. Mummy has a very long way to travel today. Have you got your toothbrush, son?" I asked, as I locked the door behind me, dropping the children's overnight bags down beside me, muttering my checklist to myself.

"Mummy, where are you going today, work again?" My daughter gave a big sigh and looked at me as if I was the worst parent in the world.

"Darling, look, I have to work, or we can't afford anything," I rolled my eyes wishing they could both cut me some slack and just be grateful I was getting them away from our awful home soon.

"You look beautiful, mummy!"

"Thank you, son." He always knew the right things to say, to defuse tension between all of us. I looked at my mirror, put my sunglasses over my tired eyes and set off to their dad's house, before my long journey to the networking event. It was on a subject that I had literally no idea about, but had been asked by the Silver Fox to meet him there, for contacts and, of course, another epic shag-athon.

"Mummy, your phone's going off." Pulling out from my street, I couldn't answer the phone and so just let it ring out. "Who's the Silver Fox?"

I turned quickly to get the phone off my daughter. "It's no one; just forget you have seen it."

"Ooh la la, Mummy has a boyfriend," she jested, singing the Kissing in a Tree song to irritate me, but I found myself smiling at her widely. "Maybe, one day." I looked at her with delight in my eyes.

"Mummy, are you in love? I thought you liked that other guy, that looks like a turnip!"

"Mum! 'He's calling again!" she screamed, over excited. I connected it to the mini and answered the call, asking the children not to make a sound.

"Good morning, young lady. Are you on your way?" His voice sounded like it was about to break into song, as it did most mornings.

"I have my children in the car, just minutes away from dropping them with their dad for the night. Can I call you back when I'm on my way?" I smiled, biting my lip.

"Oh, yes of course, that's absolutely fine L.J. If I don't answer, you know I'm with colleagues, but I will get back to you, okay?"

"Okay, looking forward to seeing you." I had wicked thoughts running around my head, about how the day and evening might unfold as we always got up to no good. I'd even worn an outfit that would be suitable for sneaking off and doing it in the car park, I was longing so much for us to sleep together again.

"I'll be seeing you soon L.J.," and he was gone, leaving me feel like I was glowing, delighted to hear his voice again and feel the excitement. Then I pulled myself together and reminded myself about our conversation last time; this was nothing more than sex.

"Mummy, he sounds so lovely. I like his voice. Marry him!" I laughed at them and pulled up outside their dad's house. I opened the door to let them both out and as they ran inside, all I could hear was them saying, "Daddy, 'Mummy's got a boyfriend." Having kissed them goodbye, I set the Satnav and dialled him back.

"Fox, can you talk?" I asked in a sexy husky voice, determined to turn him on.

"L.J. Not for long, but I'm glad you called. I'm on stand twelve; I'll be stupidly busy, and they have put me right across the corridor from my boss at the hotel. Where are you staying?"

"I'm in some shit cheap hotel again; it looks like a high-rise paradise for drug dealers. Mmmm, maybe I can sneak into your hotel room. That feels quite hot, don't you think?" I was getting wet thinking about the risk of getting caught.

"If you come to my hotel, you are going to have to be gagged young lady or do as you're fucking told, for once in your life." He laughed but was deadly serious. Knowing how much he made me scream, I couldn't argue with him.

"Fox, I'm going to be walking around about three thousand men today, in a short black dress and denim jacket, no panties and in high heels. When I get to your stand, I will drop my pen and bend over to pick it up, maybe I will even stumble, so you can accidentally lose a finger or two..." I looked ahead into the traffic. We were both silent for a few seconds and I could feel the heat between us growing.

"Fucking hell, L.J., I can feel the heat of your pussy wrapped around my cock again. I have to go. I'm getting hard and I'm with people. I will call you later," and he rang off. I took a deep breath and slumped into my seat, feeling slightly moist, lightheaded and throbbing in two places. I tried to concentrate on the road ahead but my head was flooded with emotion

Arriving at the exhibition, I checked in and was overwhelmed by the number of suits that surrounded me and the pain my heels were inevitably going to cause my feet. Clutching a map and a strong coffee, I blew my hair out of my face and set off to find him. "Fox, I'm here and I'm on route to find you." His phone went straight to voicemail, so I knew he would already be busy talking business with important people who I would have no idea how to converse with. It seemed to take forever to find him, but then there he was in front of me, talking to three rather overweight, over-paid individuals, deep in intellectual conversation, doing what he did best. A mixture of all kind of feelings hit me, all at the same time, and then there I was stood right next to him and my heart went Ring-A-Ding-Ding.

"L.J., great to see you made it. Please let me introduce you to one of my customers. This is L.J. Brown; she is one of our top recruiters," he looked at me in complete amazement and wonder. I shook his hand then turned to Fox and smiled widely.

"I can see you're busy. I don't want to interrupt your conversation; I can come back," I said apologetically, searching into his eyes. Then it happened: the moment that changed everything between us. My body felt like it was supposed to be next to his, like I'd been levelled, grounded to the spot. The only thing I could think of was that I was supposed to be by his side, always and forever and it floored me.

"L.J., are you okay?" he quizzed me worriedly searching for an answer. I had no idea where my mind and body had just gone, but I had just suddenly lost sight of my world and entered a new, unknown existence and was surprisingly very calmed by it

"I'm sorry, I'm fine. It's lovely to see you again." I didn't quite know where to put myself. I had been completely distracted by this feeling in my stomach, unlike anything I'd ever experienced before. Maybe I was going down with a bug?

"You look very beautiful and sexy, L.J.," then he bent down to my level and whispered in my ear. "Do you know, you have walked past me a few times, lost?" I looked at him, shocked, and blushed but it sounded like something I would do

"I can't read maps very well; this place is a maze. Have you been perving at me all this time?" I gave him a slightly shocked look and we both laughed quietly.

"Yes, of course I have. I've texted you twice to turn left not right, at my stand, you should check your phone." He smirked and brushed his hand across mine, not taking his eyes off me, then shook it firmly. "So, remember what I said about who you need to talk to. I've already mentioned you to a few people, so it should be very easy to network. Good luck. I want a full report on how you get on," he said confidently.

"On it, Fox!" I looked down at my phone and showed him my plan of action.

"It was nice to see you again, Miss Brown." He winked at me and shook my hand leaving a business card in it, then leant down to me to whisper in my ear.

"I'll see you tonight, when I get out of here. The hotel address is on the back of the card." I looked at him, then dropped the business card on the floor on purpose and bent over to pick it up, knowing what he could see.

"Till then, Fox." And I walked away, turning back to face him once more and I could see that he had fallen apart, watching me walk away. I smiled and he smiled shyly back at me, not taking his eyes away from me leaving him. I instantly missed him and anticipated the night ahead. "Ring-A-Ding-Fucking-Dong!" I said to myself under my breath as I walked away from him into the crowds.

Chapter Nine:
Here's to the Losers!

Exhausted from walking around endless exhibition stands and talking to every sales director on my list of new potential clients, I soon realised I had learnt nothing about the industry other than that walking around in a short dress and smiling at men sweetly, made them fall over themselves to want a client meeting and for me to do business with them. But it had helped that the top dog in the industry, had put a good word in for me. It was a male-dominated environment; I had seen very few females there and the ones I did see were recruiters, following their managers around like little puppies.

My hotel was like a scene from *The Shining*, endless long and spooky corridors. My room was on the fifth floor, right at the end of the corridor, where lights flickered and the door didn't lock properly once it was closed. Inside, the room looked so seedy, like it had possibly been used to rent out by the hour. I picked my phone up and called Fox's number, hoping for him to save me from this awful place as quickly as possible. "Fox, facetime me," I said in exasperation, then hung up.

"What is it, L.J.; are you okay?" he said alarmed, then looked at me and smiled sweetly.

"Look at this room. I can't stay here." I gave him a guided tour, including the silverfish coming out of the tap in the bathroom.

"Oh, my god, why is your boss such a cheapskate? You need to look around for another job, L.J.; he is not looking after you. I should be done by eight thirty. Get out of there, have some dinner, then bring your things to my room. I'm in a hundred and six. Text me when you're here, okay? I have to go." He made me feel safe, gave me another reassuring smile and stared into my eyes, then hung up. Throwing myself back on the bed, I gave a big sigh of relief, when my phone bleeped again. "'You did good today. People have talked to me about you. Did you get many business cards?'" I blushed at the thought of the one I had dropped on the floor and picked up.

"'Over sixty and a few compliment slips with names and numbers on. My feet hurt most of all, they need a good massage.'" I reached down and started to rub them.

"'Well, I will be giving you a good rub somewhere else in a few hours, to take your mind off it. Got to go.'"

I grinned widely and ran to the mirror. God, I looked so tired. I'd better hope the shower is safe to use, as I need to look amazing for this very naughty Fox. I decided to have a little play first, record it and send him the video, then get a shower, slip into a nice dress, then leave for his hotel.

The country roads seemed to go on forever, until I reached a very small hotel that looked like a barn conversion, with pretty fairy lights at the front entrance. Parking, I pulled my case from the boot and tried not to fall over my own feet, walking down the gravel entrance to reception. His room was on the first floor, so I got in the lift and texted him that I was there. He didn't answer, so after leaving the lift, I called. "L.J. Brown has entered the building, wearing no panties and very high heels. Where are you?" My face was lit up, in anticipation of seeing him. I literally couldn't wait to kiss him.

"I'm in my room, please be very quiet; my boss is literally across the hall from me. No panties, still?" he jested and hung up. I gently knocked at the door and he opened it to let me in, rushing me through. He immediately looked me in the eye and locked his hand behind my head, then kissed me passionately and hard. We both fell over my case and landed on the bed giggling.

"God you look good." He kissed me again, like he had missed me for a thousand years. Rolling me onto my back, he pushed me down to the bed, putting his fingers inside me, letting me feel how hard he was. Then he started to tear off my clothes like an animal, breaking my bra and tossing it onto the floor.

"Someone is in a rush tonight," I whispered, biting his lip. He was then inside me, kissing me hard and I could feel how hard he was and how full he'd made me.

"God, Fox, slow down. 'You'll cum too soon." Putting his fingers to my mouth, to stop me talking, he pulled out and stood up, asking me with his eyes, to do the same. In front of us there was a massive mirror on the wall. I looked down and could see his familiar car keys and business cards with a mixture of new ones he'd picked up from the exhibition.

"Look at your body. Don't talk, just keep watching us in the mirror." He kissed my neck and squeezed my breast, running his hands down my body, like he was following a map. My eyes followed his face and what his hands were doing to me. "Look at what we look like together. Look at your body L.J.; it's unbelievably sexy. Your bottom is perfect and your breasts... you don't get much better than this." He turned me around and kissed me again. I didn't speak, as instructed; it was quite hot letting him take complete control of me and me not coming out with usual complete shit that often got me into trouble. "Wine?" he asked. I nodded and he began to pour the wine into our glasses. I looked in the mirror at myself again and touched my body without him but making him aware of what I was doing. Tossing my hair to one side, I bent over and stuck my butt in the air, then turned my head to look at him.

"Fuck me, Fox," I said wickedly, not taking my eyes off him. He glugged some wine and came closer to me, rubbing the wetness of my clit up and down, slowly, knowing exactly what to do and looking like he'd never looked before. He was lost in the moment and so focused on me, that the passion between us literately made me cum in seconds.

Standing back up, I walked towards him and grabbed my glass of wine, drinking it slowly. I touched his face and kissed his nose. Handing him the glass back, I instructed him what to do without even having to say a word. He flipped me around and entered me from behind, pounding into me, grabbing my hair, so my face had to look towards the mirror. God, we looked good. As he grabbed my breast and pushed deep inside me, I couldn't help but moan. He covered my mouth with his hand, and it became too intense to bear. I bit into him and we both came so hard, watching each other in the mirror, our expressions never to be forgotten. Pulling me back, he stayed inside me for minutes and kissed me gently, out of breath and spent, then pulled out and we both reached for our wine, drinking in silence.

I flopped down onto the bed and he joined me. I flipped over onto my front and he ran his fingers up and down my back, while I drank my wine and recovered. We could never stop touching each other and hardly took our eyes off each other.

"Look, L.J., we need to talk. Well, whisper." He turned to me, with a concerned expression and I was instantly worried.

"Of course, what is it?" I drank my wine, thinking he was going to ask me something about work, that I probably could answer.

"I don't want you to take this the wrong way, but there's no love inside me." I was not expecting this at all and immediately shot upright in bed and paid attention.

"What do you mean?" I asked, worried, my heart beating at a million miles an hour, thinking the absolute worst.

"My heart is black. I don't have feelings and I don't want to." He looked completely different; his expression was much harder, and I didn't recognise the person in front of me anymore. Pulling the bed sheet over me to cover myself up, I moved slightly away, and my mind flashed back to the Millionaire Strawberry Psycho. I was going to get murdered for sure, but this time after sex and in a hotel room, where I can't escape, because of his big fatheaded boss.

"So, what are you saying to me, Fox?" I didn't even bother to whisper and was defensive immediately.

"I've read your book, and I know how much fun you like. I can handle that, but I'm incapable of anything else. I care about my children and that's all." He looked scared that I might hit him and got out of bed to put his pants back on.

"Okay, well I guess that's fine," I replied after a long pause. "I knew we were just having fun, it's no big deal." I looked into my wine glass and ran my fingers around the rim.

"L.J., this is not about you. I think you are amazing, beautiful, clever and you're possibly going to be a millionaire when your book comes out. You can have anyone you want, and I know you still think about Mr Fancy Pants. You talk about him quite a bit!" I looked shocked at his mention of Fancy Pants.

"It's over between Fancy Pants and me. You know that." I looked at him with dishonest eyes and we both knew it wasn't true.

"I will get my things and go then," I said, as I tried to hold back the tears, thinking that I'd read every signal wrong and that even he knew I'd never fully give myself to another man, as long as Fancy Pants was alive and well. He knew me and he was being honest about himself and the combination crushed me so hard, I felt sick.

"No, you can't go. 'Don't be silly; you've had a drink. I'm quite happy to continue with this. I just need you to know where we stand; it's just fun. If you can cope with that, then, well, we will have a fantastic time. I'm just not in a great place, work, kids... I have a lot going on. You are the same too. You need to find your feet in life L.J. Let this be something to blow off steam. I can help you in your career." I pulled myself close to him and put my head on his chest staring across the room away from him.

"I guess you're right," I said, with no emotion, completely lost. So much was going around in my head, the very fact that I liked him had scared me in the first place and this new information had shocked me even more. My mind drifted to that old familiar place of utter confusion.

What the fuck am I doing with him anyway? He is older than me and I can't stand his ties. He cuts me off all the time when I am talking to him on the phone and he just let me fall for him and all along he was using me for sex. When I wake up in the morning, I'll be gone before him and never see him again.

"L.J., are you okay?" He kissed and stroked the back of my head.

"I'm completely fine, Fox. 'You're totally right; I do still have feelings for Fancy Pants. I need to go to sleep... long trip home in the morning." I downed the wine, grabbed the bottle, filled my glass again and disappeared to the bathroom. I drank it down fast, looking in the mirror at my face, knowing that I was back to square one, no man's land. No one loves me or wants me and probably never will. I toasted myself in the mirror, "Cheers to being such a loser. How did I not see it? What a fucking idiot!"

Returning to the room, I turned the lights out and got back into bed with him. He turned to talk, but I said I was tired, and that his boss might hear us, then fell asleep.

Chapter Ten:
How Little it Matters, How Little We Know

I woke up with him still beside me in bed, and he opened his eyes. Not saying anything at all, I climbed on top of him seductively and began to make love my way. He pushed my legs under him and thrust his hips forward, for maximum feel good factor. Looking into each other's eyes and not knowing what the hell either of us were doing, we slowly came at the same time, blowing my head off with intensity, then rolled back next to each other, cuddling in silence. Was this a goodbye from me, or a confirmation that I could allow this to continue?

"I have to get out of here, L.J. I've got the room tonight again, so stay as long as you need; have a shower and a coffee." He was back to being sweet again; the coldness in his voice, that I had heard last night, had disappeared. I watched him get up and disappear to the shower, got out of bed and grabbed my phone.

"Are we still on for tonight, to do the final edit?" I'd had a message from Maureen, asking if our girls night/edit was still going ahead. Texting back quickly that it was, I realised how much I'd had to drink and probably needed a few hours more sleep. I had a full night of hard work ahead. I got up and went to the bathroom, I'd heard him get into the shower, so I knocked on the door and asked if it was okay to brush my teeth. As I watched him in the shower from the mirror, he began to sing Sinatra. I loved listening to him; he had so much confidence and a great voice. I smiled at him and he asked me to join him. Kissing and singing in the shower, we washed each other, had a little play and got out. Still wet, he bent me over in front of the mirror, wiped away the steam and fucked me hard, so I could watch again. This time we both smiled as we watched. The agreement had been made; we were officially fucking, with no emotions, no strings attached. Until we got bored, I guessed. We had not discussed it, but this seemed to be the case most of the time, our body language was doing all the work.

"Harder, Fox. Harder! He bent me down further, so my head was near the sink, almost banging against it. Slipping around on the wet floor, he pounded into me and screamed out as he came so hard, I felt the cum explode inside me and saw his orgasm in his face. "Fox, I'm not there. You need to carry on." He looked at me with devilment and I was hungry for the build-up and explosion he would create inside me. He took me to a full-length mirror, got down on his knees, looked directly at me and told me to watch. My legs shook and I had to hold on to the wall, as he teased me with his tongue and fingers until I squirted all over him, then he pushed me down on the bed and fucked me, until I came another four times.

"Satisfied young lady?" he asked, kissing me. I rolled my eyes and smiled widely.

"No, do it again!" I laughed into his mouth and grabbed his penis, so he couldn't get away.

"Mmmmm, L.J., there is nothing more I would like to do, than be inside you, all day every day, but I have to go to work." He kissed me one more time and then got back in the shower, singing again.

After getting out of the shower he got dressed and chatted away about business and my plans for the weekend. I told him about the final edit, and he became excited for me. "Good girl, when's the release date?" He looked distracted, trying to tie one of his awful ties.

"July twenty-seventh has been given to me as a rough date, it's just eight weeks away."

"And your meeting with them, when is that?" he quizzed, knowing that we would be able to meet up again.

"A week on Friday. I'm taking a pitstop on the way back to fuck you stupid, if that's alright?" I jested, smirking at him and opening my legs, so he could see me playing. He leaned down, licked from my asshole to my clit slowly and I was lost for words. It was seriously sexy, and I wanted him immediately.

"Sounds like a plan to me. Just let me know when and where." He looked at me naked on the bed and pointed to his penis. "Look what you've done!" He grabbed his jacket, keys and cards and looked at me one more time as he reached for the door. "Drive safely home and call me in a few hours." He looked me in the eyes for what seemed too long, came back to kiss me quickly, then he was gone. Ignorance is bliss. 'We're just two tingles that intermingle, so why do I need to define it? Who knows what love is anyway? Why would I want this fun to go away? I curled back up under the sheets and could still smell his aftershave on the pillow next to me. I cuddled up to it, but instantly missed him and felt sad. Unsure of what my head and heart were doing to me right now, I fell back to sleep.

Chapter Eleven:
The Impossible Dream

I had to drive only a few miles to get to where I needed to be to edit the book, but I got completely lost. My navigation skills were so bad, even with a satnav. Finally arriving, I parked up and carried out my overnight things and a bottle of wine. When I pressed the buzzer to the flat, it was answered with excited greetings, and I was on my way up the stairs to her apartment in no time at all. Walking through the door, I was welcomed and offered a drink and food immediately. Throwing their arms around me, Maureen and Sally, my old work friends, were giddy and chatting about the book and how much fun they had been having reading it. We were all set for a night of editing and drinking.

It had been so long since I'd seen them, having worked with them for the same company when I had just finished university nearly nineteen years ago. We were still in contact and very good friends through social media. Maureen and Sally were senior to me by almost twenty years, but very liberal and forward thinking. "Ladies, are you ready for this?" I laughed, raising a glass of wine. and we all said, "Cheers to tiramisu!"

"L.J., you are so bad; I can't believe what I have read. I have so many questions. You do realise there are a lot of errors?"

I looked concerned and then admitted to my lack of ability, "I'm fucking useless at spelling; I'm surprised I passed GCSE English, but this book just poured out of me. I literally couldn't stop it." I looked down at my glass, "I just have to take a gamble, ladies. People will either love it or hate it. Whatever happens, happens, bad punctuation and all."

"I agree. Nothing ventured, nothing gained. Reach for the stars." Maureen cheered.

"Okay, so the dedications are not in yet. Have you thought about what you would like to put? Are you dedicating it to Fancy Pants and your love affair with him?" Maureen asked, dying for an insight into my mind and pouring more wine into my glass.

I have to dedicate it to all my friends and family for putting up with me. I was totally pissed writing absolutely all of it, plus I ate a few million servings of tiramisu, so that has to go in for giggles." I laughed, and they raised their glasses to me again. "But I was so sad and so lost. I've obviously written the book as a way of coping with my emotions. I didn't know what the hell was going on, or how to process any of it." I looked at them both with tears in my eyes, and they knew.

"I did discuss the dedication with Fancy Pants, to try to make him like me more, I guess, but there is no way in the world he should get a mention; he's treated me so badly." I sighed and sat back in my chair.

"What's his problem? I can't believe he just picks you up and drops you all the time," Sally said with disgust. "I know it's harsh, L.J., but he's just used you for sex. You do realise this don't you? You might have had incredible sex, but is he worth any more of your time?"

I looked at her and fell deep into thought. "He's a narcissist and I think I have worked out that I am a co-dependant, so together we are completely toxic. He feeds off me, I feed off him and we go around in circles." I bit my lip and felt my heart pound because I knew what he was and what I was doing and still didn't want to fully admit it to myself.

"Let me google 'narcissist'," and I'll show you what it means. Then you can see the patterns that form in the book. He's a predator and people like me are easy targets. Newly divorced, single mums, no self-esteem, no confidence. He made me feel like I was the most amazing woman on the planet, then pulled me apart until there was nothing left of me, so he could feel good. Worst thing is, he didn't and still doesn't realise he is doing it." I looked for YouTube clips of narcissistic behaviour and showed them both. "Mr Philosopher told me about this, over and over again, but I didn't want to hear it. I thought I was in love and I might have been, but he is really bad news for me.

"So, I guess this book is a real-life example of what can happen and how a person's mind can be completely taken over by crazy obsession."

"Oh my god, L.J., do you need to go and see a counsellor, to help you get over him?" Giving me a hug, she looked so concerned as we read the information off the screen.

"Look at this: 'narcissism is a mental condition, in which a person has an inflated sense of their own importance.' 'Narcissists have a deep need for excessive attention and admiration; they experience troubled relationships and lack of empathy for others.' See, it's spot on." The wine was starting to kick in and I was becoming animated.

"Well, L.J., he's definitely in love with himself, that's for sure. I can't believe what I'm reading here; this explains so much," Maureen said, shocked at the realisation.

"'Exaggerated sense of self,'" I continued, "'excessive admiration, superior and manipulating. Expects special favours', (like getting me to send naughty videos) 'and unquestioning compliance with their expectations.' (I wouldn't dare NOT do it for him.) 'Takes advantage of others, to get what they want and has a total inability or unwillingness to recognise the needs and feelings of others.'" I questioned the last part as he seemed to be a good dad at least. "But read this, it will scare the shit out of you." I scrolled down further. "'At the same time, people with narcissistic personality disorder have trouble handling anything they perceive as criticism, they can then become impatient or angry, react with rage, ultimately it could make him very ill.' Not that I should care, he's such a fucking dick head, I'm really starting to hate him." I clicked off the page and grabbed my wine. They both looked shocked and worried for me.

"It probably didn't help that I called him a wanker pants most of the time, did it?" I laughed and tried to lighten the mood.

"You need to lose contact with this man; it could become dangerous L.J." They both reached over to hold my hand and reassure me.

"Why I was attracted to and maintained a relationship with a narcissist is interesting also, look at this." I sprang to my feet again grabbing my laptop. "I think I am what you might call a co-dependent. I wanted to make him happy. It was a challenge to me to make him happy, but when I couldn't figure it out, I became obsessed with him. I couldn't understand what I was doing wrong." I shrugged my shoulders, still not really understanding it all.

"I'm like a fly to shit with him. He could completely trash my existence and I would still go back because I was addicted to his constant approval. It's apparently human nature, to try to fix things we don't understand. So technically I'm quite normal." I turned my laptop so they could see, and I saw their faces drop in acknowledgement, as I read on. "'A narcissist needs what is referred to as their narcissistic supply, which comes from the co-dependant. This is a desperate attempt to avoid self-loathing and deep insecurity that most people with this condition feel at their core. It's a completely toxic cycle of behaviour and psychological abuse that can literally go on for a lifetime, if you don't stop it.'" I closed my eyes and felt the torture, knowing I still wasn't ready to give up on him and I still felt like I could fix him, but deep down I knew it was completely pointless.

"Right ladies, enough of the depressing heavy crap, at least I had great sex and you have to admit it will make people laugh." I winked and poured another glass. "We need to get to work before I'm totally pissed and incapable of understanding my own writing."

"Okay, L.J. Well, I have a question. It's mentioned repeatedly in the book and I have absolutely no idea what it means." I looked interested and ready to answer any questions. "What's squirting?" Sally looked down her glasses at me and started to type on her computer to look it up. I bolted out of my seat to stop her, not able to contain my uncomfortable laughter.

"Okay, ladies, it's time for a bit of sex education!"

Chapter Twelve:
Bang, Bang (My Baby Shot Me Down)

"L.J., will you concentrate!" I looked across the room, out of breath, my heart pounding in my chest from so much physical exercise. I acknowledge my instructor's comment. "Six more on the punch bag, then move to the ball. Got it?" he bellowed at me and looked at me with his unwavering eyes, telling me to get with the programme.

'Fucking have it!' I thought to myself, punching the shit out of the sandbag. You're such an asshole, Fancy Pants, I hate you. I hate you more than I've ever hated anyone in my life. Thinking you can use me and get away with it. How do you sleep at night knowing you're a giant cockhead? Processing all the information I now knew from my research and blatant evidence, I was angry, but if I was truthful, mostly angry with myself for letting it happen to me in the first place.

Punch! Kick…! Aggressively I hit and kicked the sandbag six more times. My cardiovascular workout was just what I needed today. I needed to release some tension and anger, even if I don't like the class much. Why could I not have been gay? I daydreamed that I would never have to deal with men ever again. Anyway, I don't need anyone to make me feel complete, I can do this by myself, right? But, what if I can't? What if I am co-dependant? Does this mean I'm going to continue to be lost forever, in a whirlpool of chaos? What childhood stuff has happened that's made me so messed up? It seemed normal to me, other than my parent's' separation. I don't understand any of it; nothing makes sense!

"L.J., move!" I jumped out of my skin as my instructor screamed at me. "Skipping rope!" I looked at him embarrassed and red in the face, sweat pouring off me, and picked the skipping rope up from the floor. Skip. Jump. Repeat. I could never get the rhythm right. I used to be able to do this at school; why was it so hard as an adult? I was a tangled mess but tried my hardest. Co-dependant means lost, loss of self. How did I get lost? How do I even know how to find me again and where do I start?

"Three, two, one, next ladies!" Running across the room, burning with heat, I picked up a ball bigger than me and held it out at arm's length. God it hurt. It was pink and it made me giggle for a second, as I thought of playing with the Fox's balls last week and telling him to get a wax. Holding the ball away from my chest I calmed my breathing down and my arms began to shake. Looking into the distance, I could see all the others working hard, being focused and looking like they were in control of their life. I felt very sad, lonely and insecure. I didn't know what I wanted to do with my career, but it certainly wasn't recruiting. I felt like I was running out of time and options. No one seemed to understand me, but how can I expect anyone to, if I don't even understand myself?

I looked ahead of me and there was a poster on the wall saying, 'I hated every minute of training, but I said, "Don't quit. Suffer now and live the rest of your life a champion." 'Muhammad Ali.' Tears welled up in my eyes as I knew I was close to breaking point and needed some inner strength to get me though this somehow. I couldn't let my children down, so I had no option but to move forward into a better place. If only people knew how insecure I was. I hated the way I looked, so I changed myself all the time. I thought I was stupid and I was terrible at my job. I found bringing up my kids a massive challenge and I felt like I was failing at it. I was in debt and went hungry to feed the children. What was there that was good in my life other that I was alive and my kids were healthy? I supposed I should be completely grateful for that though. I pretended to the world that I had the most amazing life ever and that everything was under control 'Ms Big Shot I've written a book and have an amazing sex life.' It was all crap to make myself feel better.

I'd told so many people I'd written this book, what if it flopped? I'd be a laughingstock. Truth was, I wanted to get off the rollercoaster, meet a nice man, fall in love and share my life with him. God, my head was exploding with negative thoughts, I hated this spiral.

"Bikes! L.J., concentrate! You're not here to daydream!" I dropped the ball and it bounced halfway around the gym, sending me running after it. Mounting the bike and getting dizzy, I sat back, drank some water and paused for a few minutes to collect myself.

"Stand up, position one." I gave my instructor a pathetic look of defeat; I was dying. I was super unfit, and I had smoked too many cigarettes and drunk too much wine to cope with this level of exercise.

The instructor came over to my bike stared into my eyes with intensity. "Fight through it, L.J. Fight!" He gave me a look of confidence, winked and then moved away. Tipping my head down, he instructed me to turn the lever halfway and then I was climbing. Pushing through the pain and not giving up, I was nearly in tears. "Breathe in, breathe out," he instructed. I focused so I didn't pass out. Thinking to myself over and over, I could change my life and make it better, I know I could. I couldn't think about

Fancy Pants anymore. I needed to find out what it is I had to do for work. I hated my job even if it did mean I got to see the Fox and have fun. I needed to be happy; I needed to find out what I really wanted.

There was no way I was going to accept that I was lost. Only I could do this; I had the power! Fuck men. I had the Silver Fox; he was a fantastic guy, who gave me support. I knew he didn't want anything serious, but right now he was exactly what I needed: a distraction away from Mr Knobhead of the year! Someone kind for a change, someone that had time for me, someone that turned me on and didn't fuck me off.

You don't get to win Fancy Pants! You might have tipped me over the edge and pulled me down, so I didn't know who I was anymore, but I won't let you destroy me. You were nothing but a worm, a pathetic one at that. Oh, and the little insecurity you had about your penis being small, I'm afraid you were right, it was probably on par with your heart a shrivelled up, dysfunctional body part.

"Great class, ladies. See you next week." Before I knew it, the class had come to an end. The instructor came over to the bikes and gave everyone high fives, except me. "You okay, L.J? You're not your sparkly self today." He looked slightly concerned but still tried to be hard.

"Yes, I'm fine. I'm just getting over a scumbag."
I stood up tall and proud, my legs wobbling slightly
as I tried to stop myself from falling over. He reached
for a hug and I pushed him away. "I wouldn't, I
stink!" Something had just changed inside me. I had
reached a crossroads and was not going to stop until
I found out which direction I needed to go.

Chapter Thirteen:
Stay with Me...

Everything was packed apart from my faithful old laptop; taking one final look around the dungeon and bidding farewell to the resident ghost, damp, and smelly cooker, I felt more positive about life. I powered up my laptop, sat on the floor and contemplated my future. I was out of here and would never let myself live in this state again. Just one last thing to do now, I thought to myself; opening my emails, I attached the full book and wrote an email to my publisher.

Dear Pegasus,

Attached is my final edited version of the book. I look forward to our meeting next week. I have so many ideas for advertising it.

Let's kick Fifty Shades off the shelves to make some room for a slice of Tiramisu! 😊

Regards,

L.J. x

Springing to my feet, I heard a knock at the door and the removal van was outside ready to load my boxes. Moving to somewhere new and exciting, a complete fresh start, was just what I needed. I knew it wouldn't take long to move. I didn't have many things and the drive was only an hour away, so I was hoping for it all to be moved in one trip.

I'd already had a million calls and one of them was from the magic Fox, so I decided to call him back first, while I was beaming with excitement. "Fox, you called?" I pointed to a few boxes and smiled apologetically at the removal men for being on my phone, when they asked me what needed to go in first.

"Young lady, are you still happy for me to take a trip up to Yooorkshire?" I laughed down the phone at his interpretation; he always took the mickey out of my accent.

"By 'eck now, that'd be reet nice, Fox," I said in a heavy Yorkshire twang and grinned widely, biting my lip and twiddling my hair.

"Okay, I'll be up north tonight to celebrate your move, but I can't stay; I need to drive back down south I'm afraid. Plus, I'm fully aware that after seven p.m. Yorkshire has no electricity and will be in candle light," he jested warmly.

"Fox, I'm going to need wine and lots of it. Oh, and we need to discuss a few candidates I think you might want to see for your sales job, before I leave that awful company." I tried to make him feel I'd not forgotten about his pressing need for staff.

"I'll pick you up from your new address at eight p.m. I have to take a call. Have fun moving and I'll see you tonight" and he was gone, and time was now my issue.

After a long day of moving and some unpacking, I had a bed made up and a functional bathroom and kitchen, but boxes were everywhere, and I suddenly realised how small the new house was. There was no sign of dirt or mould, no awful smells and a fantastic private little back garden with an apple tree. I fell back onto the sofa, looked all around and relaxed my body; peace at last and somewhere my kids would be happy. I smiled and felt sleepy instantly, but dragged myself off the sofa and upstairs, jumping into my new clean shower with no pervert ghost to watch me. Feeling the warm water clean my skin, I listened to the music on my phone play list and danced around like a child.

My phone kept ringing, stopping the music, so I grabbed my towel, got out and answered it. It was Fox. I hung up and facetimed him, then got back in the shower with my phone away from the water but facing towards my naked body. "Fox, I don't usually get many calls in the shower, but since it's you…" I grinned at him and slowly took him on a guided tour of my body pushing soap around and down between my legs.

"L.J., that's very naughty! You're in then? All unpacked? He coughed awkwardly, and I knew I'd made him instantly hard.

"I'm in, but no way near unpacked. How far away are you?" I rubbed some soap on my breast and squeezed the nipple so he could see, slowly and seductively biting my lip.

"My cock's rock-hard, L.J.," his voice had changed and was now deep and husky. I loved his sexy voice; it turned me on so much. I closed my eyes and reached between my legs, letting him watch.

"I'm pulling over; you're going to make me crash," he gasped. I played for a few minutes before my arm started to get tired holding the phone away, then teased him by blowing a kiss and hanging up.

Getting out of the shower, I found some towels packed in a box clearly labelled bathroom and was amazed that I'd been so organised. That feeling of control over everything was starting to come back to me; I was in a better place in my head. New house, with a possible idea for a new job, although at least I did have one, and I had this nice sexy man, who was extremely good in bed and, it would seem, quite into me. My phone rang again.

"I'm twenty minutes away. I will wait in the car outside." He sounded frustrated and as though he couldn't get to me fast enough.

"But I'm not ready," I said alarmed. "Can you not come in first?" I'd hoped he would ravish me, when I answered the door wearing only my towel.

"Erm okay. I will come in, but only if you let me play with your pussy." I blushed and danced around on the spot.

"He's not in right now; he's probably out chasing pussy himself," I joked with him, running around tripping over things, attending to my hair and makeup.

"What are you wearing right now?" he asked lustfully.

"Right now, nothing at all, Mr Silver fucking get here faster Fox. I'm going to jump on your naughty massive cock!"

"Oh my god, I can feel the heat of your pussy wrapped around my cock," he said, blowing my mind and making me nearly drop my phone down the toilet.

"Drive faster, Fox. I'm waiting," I moaned down the phone, playing, and hung up.

He knocked at my door and let himself in, welcoming me full of smiles, taking my face in his hands, kissing me hard, not even paying attention to my messy house or what I was wearing. It was still light outside and the sun shone onto my back through the kitchen window, where he had pinned me against the kitchen unit. I felt his hard cock press into me, and I grabbed it and squeezed it gently in acknowledgement.

"Fuck me Fox. I've had a very hard day." I looked at him wide eyed. He picked me up and carried me across the room to the stairs, then put me down and chased me, following my direction to my room, smacking my ass. Standing up, undressing each other, kissing and laughing, the passion between us both was so intense, I felt like I was going dizzy from my endorphins coursing through my body. We fell onto the bed and kissed each other everywhere until we couldn't take it any longer and then he was inside me, deep and hard, but slowly, never taking his eyes off me.

"The shower facetime was a very naughty thing to do, Miss Brown." He pushed back the hair from my face that had got tangled everywhere.

"I like feeling wet, Fox. 'It's one of my favourite things." I searched his face and he rammed into me.

"I can't tell," he whispered into my ear and thrust again and again and again, making me scream. He stroked my face and asked to use the bathroom, kissing my nose and getting up.

"We haven't cum yet," I questioned him, surprised that he had just stopped.

"Patience young lady, I've just driven two hundred miles and I need the bathroom; we have lots of time." He winked and left the room.

I shouted, "Grab the champagne from the sink!" I'd left it in cold water to chill, as my fridge was not cold enough yet. "'But don't ask me where the glasses are," I continued to bellow out, then laid there waiting for him, listening for him coming back up the steps and my heart began to race.

"Well, I found this lying about. Have you been having naughty dreams again?" He held a massive cucumber in one hand and the bottle of champagne in the other.

"Everyone needs cucumber practice," I shrugged my shoulders and giggled at his reference to my book; I knew now he had paid attention.

"I didn't see any oranges, but you can squeeze mine if you like, guaranteed not to explode just yet." Smirking, he handed me the cucumber and began to open the champagne. "Here's to your new start." He popped the cork and handed me the bottle; I gave it a quick swig and handed it back to him.

"Cheers!" I raised my hand with the cucumber still in it, distracting his eyes away from me for a moment.

"Have you ever used one for pleasure, L.J?" he quizzed.

"No! It was just a silly dream and I wanted to turn readers on. It seemed fun at the time." I blushed at the thought of it.

"Can I use it with you? Just to see what it's like for both of us?" I looked shocked, but then thought that it was no different than using a dildo, so with my eyes, I agreed.

He slowly pulled me to the edge of the bed and knelt down on the floor, going down on me he teased me and licked me and played with me, until I was close to cumming, then stopped. Slowly, he pushed his cucumber inside me, but it wouldn't fit (Flash back to a time with Mr Fancy Pants, when he took my anal virginity).

"It's not going to fit, Fox. And god, fuck, it's very cold!" I panicked a little and then laid my head back down.

"Relax," he said in his deep sexy voice. I felt a pinch and it was in. It felt harder than a cock, not as comfortable as a dildo and very cold and unusual. Then I looked at him, at what he was doing, propping a pillow behind my head so I could watch more comfortably. His face was motionless, like he was lost in a world of his own, this turned me on so much I soon began to build and to my surprise, I squirted everywhere, covering him and my sheets.

"Fucking hell, Fox. Get inside me. Now!" I screamed, grabbing him on top of me and he was inside me within seconds. We pounded into each other like animals, throwing each other around the bed, pinning each other down and fucking like our lives depended on it, until we both came at the same time, screaming out each other's names and finally collapsing in a heap.

"Pass me the champagne please, Fox," I said breathlessly. He passed it to me, and I handed it back so he could have some more too. "Do you think they used vegetables and fruit before vibrators were invented?" I burst out laughing and kissed him hard. "I'm sure the jolly green giant might get a kick out of corn being used, ribbed for her pleasure," I continued now, on a role with my jokes, laughing so hard I was almost crying.

"I know what they used as a cup before one was invented," he turned to me and pushed me onto my back. Grabbing a pillow, he placed it underneath my bottom and pulled my legs apart. My heart was racing in anticipation of what he was going to do next. Slowly he poured some champagne inside my pussy, it trickled down the sides and he put his mouth around it to drink. Not taking his eyes off me, he licked everywhere, then worked his way up my body to my belly button and filled that too and drank out of it.

"Kiss me, Fox!" I demanded desperately. His head went back between my legs and then slowly he moved his way up to my mouth, kissed me and once again was inside me.

"I'm going to cum again, L.J. I'm sorry," he said nervously.

"Pull out. I want you to cum all over me, Fox." But it was too late. He was spent, on top of me and panting.

"Wow! Wow! Wow!" was all we could say to each other.

"I wish we could just stay like this forever," I sighed and turned to kiss him, but he said nothing back. We rested in each other's arms, before getting up to go out.

Chapter Fourteen:
Call Me Irresponsible...

We had a quick shower together, kissing, talking and giggling with each other. Then we got dressed, left the house, and jumped into the car, setting off into the beautiful countryside.

"Are you okay to drive?" I questioned, feeling a little lightheaded from the champagne, squinting at the sun setting and reaching for my shades in my bag.

"I think most of it went in you and on the bed Mrs." He smiled wide eyed and set off.

"Do you know where we are going, or are we just going to have a drive and see where we end up?" His eyes gleamed with excitement and wonder, heading into the middle of nowhere.

Finally, finding a lovely remote little pub in the middle of the Yorkshire Dales, we pulled up and I kissed him before getting out of the car. Everything was stimulated, my body, my mind and my heart. I was in such an unusual place.

"Come on, you sexy fucker, I need to get pissed."

I darted out of the car and he followed me, putting his hand up my skirt, making me jump.

"Largemerlot, for the lady," he ordered without even asking me. I nodded, impressed and in agreement, while he ordered a lemonade. We wandered to the other side of the pub where we could sit and kiss like teenagers, with no one watching us or interrupting. The room was filled with large oak tables that backed on to a beer garden. To the left of me there was an old piano and some wicker baskets filled with wood for the open fire. I could smell the freshly cut grass outside, but it was too cold to sit in the garden area. My mind told me I was hungry, but I had gone passed eating and just wanted to drink and hold him.

"God, Fox, we need air," I gasped.

"I've got a hard on in a pub, L.J." He looked at me, shocked, grabbing a menu to hide it.

"Well, don't waste it," I said in a sexy devious voice, "Why don't we just do it here; no one's watching." I put my hand underneath the menu and inside his pants to feel him growing.

"L.J., stop it!" He turned to me shocked. "Anyone could walk in." He pulled my hand away.

"What? There is no one here; it's dead. We could do it on that piano. Would you sing Sinatra to me again?" I teased him and kissed him, grabbing the back of his head and running my fingers through his hair.

"You have had too much to drink. Have you eaten today?" he looked concerned.

"Nope, only breakfast." I swigged the wine down and gestured for a refill. He shook his head and set off back to the bar, so I disappeared to the toilets to refresh myself. The wine had gone to my head and I was super horny, worse than usual. Although I'd only just had sex an hour ago, I wanted to go again.

"Are you okay?" He looked at me worriedly and handed me the wine reluctantly, meeting me at the bar and walking back to our table.

"'I'm fine!" I said loudly, raising the heads of people sitting in the pub, making them pay attention to us and stare disapprovingly. "Fox, it's full of stiffs in here. We need to get out of here and find somewhere to fuck". He put his hand over my mouth to shut me up, looking at me with wondering eyes, not knowing quite what to do or say.

"Let's just have our drinks and then I'll take you home, young lady; the day has caught up with you. I haven't seen you like this since we first met, that night in the hotel room." We sat back down and began to kiss again, banging into each other's teeth and pulling away laughing, then we talked about the day and how much fun it had been.

"Let me give you a blow job, Fox. No one can see, and it would turn me on; the thought of being caught is super naughty." I was deadly serious and didn't have a care in the world.

"Crazy girl, let's get out of here. Maybe don't finish your wine?" He took it out of my hand and put it down on the table. I picked it back up and finished it, watching him, and shrugged my shoulders. "Right, I'm taking you home. What's gotten into you?" He touched my face and kissed me but looked really concerned.

"I'm celebrating my move, I said, putting my hands in the air, being too loud for a small county pub. He grabbed my hand and led me out to the car, putting our glasses on the bar and saying thank you to the staff.

"Fox, I'm drunk!" I said, animatedly, leaning over to him, resting my head on his shoulder while he set off driving. He looked at me looking at him with my big blue eyes and a massive grin. "'Let's have sex again!" Loosening my seat belt, I leaned over and began to undo his belt and fly, getting his hard cock out for me to play with. I didn't need to say anything, he knew exactly what I wanted to do. I looked at him, then positioned my body towards him and went down on him in the car.

"Fucking hell, L.J! Oh my god!" He let out air from his mouth and tried hard to concentrate on driving.

"Fox," I said coming up for air, "find somewhere we can't be found and let's fuck." I went back down on him and continued to make him moan until he was close, then he made me stop, before pulling up near a field where cows surrounded us. "Look, they have all come to watch," I giggled, hiccupping.

"Get out of the car," he ordered, and we both looked at each other, unbuckled and rushed to open our doors. Looking over the car at each other intensely, I staggered in my heels in the mud, to his side and he grabbed my waist pulling me into him, so I could feel what I had just done to him.

We didn't talk; we didn't need to. He slowly turned me away from him, bending me over, pulling my skirt up to my waist, dropping my panties, keeping my heels and my top on. "Don't make any noise," he whispered in my ear. I bobbed my head in agreement, hardly able to contain myself with lust and with one thrust he was inside me, against the car.

Moooo, was all we could hear from cows in the field next to us. It was like they were celebrating or congratulating us with applause at our outdoor adventure.

"Fox, stop!" I screamed, almost about to cum. He was fucking me gently, but with perfect rhythm and he wasn't going to stop until we both came. I pulled away and moved to the side of the car.

Looking at him intently, I began to completely undress, throwing my clothes everywhere.

"L.J., 'get dressed. Don't you dare!" he said, now cross.

"My panties are coming off my ankles, Fox!" I grinned like a child and tossed them in the air, doing a star jump. I watched him looking away from me and running towards the field. It was like watching a movie in slow motion, as he jumped in the air after my panties, they missed his hand and landed on a cow's head; it bolted immediately and ran away into the field. "Poor farmer's wife." I creased up laughing at the situation.

Completely naked, I walked towards him, to kiss him and start again. "*Get* dressed and *get* in the car," he ordered coldly. I was taken aback by him and looked at him as he fastened up his pants. Picking up my clothes that were scattered around, I got dressed and slowly walked round to the car to join him. We sat in the car in silence for what seemed like forever.

"What's the matter? I thought we were having fun," I blurted out, feeling insecure.

"You're drunk, and I could lose my licence. What were you thinking getting completely naked, L.J?" he said angrily.

"I thought you'd be turned on by it. I didn't think; it was just spontaneous. No one would have found us; we're in the middle of nowhere," I said defensively and confused.

"It was irresponsible," he said assertively, "You didn't think about both of us."

I turned to him and looked at him, like I had no idea who he was. "We are always irresponsible, Fox. I thought you got a kick out of fun?" I gulped, yelling at him. We were having a fight.

"Don't you shout at me!" he bellowed back.

"Well don't talk to me like I'm some sort of slag," I shouted back.

"I have never treated you or talked to you like a slag!" He raised his voice yet again.

"Well, you just did!" I folded my arms and looked out of the window. Everything was passing by so fast; I was so drunk.

"'You're just like Fancy Pants. You've used me for sex and now you're fucking me off!" the words just came from nowhere and as soon as I'd said them, I regretted it and then was thrown forward in my seat as he slammed on the brakes.

"Don't you dare tar me with the same brush as that man!" He looked at me furiously, putting the car back into first gear, sitting in silence until it was broken by my uncontrollable tears. "Stop crying, L.J.," he said firmly. I felt vulnerable and lost again, like all the time Shitty Pants had had his way and then discarded me like trash. He pulled into my driveway and we sat apart, the perfect day had turned into a nightmare because I'd had too much to drink and my true emotions had come out at the first sign of rejection.

"It's over, Fox," I said, still looking out of the window emotionless. Trying to fight the tears or show him any affection, too many people had made me sad and I knew I was falling hard and fast for him, so it had to end now before I fell in love.

"No! No, L.J., it's not. Come on, you know you mean more to me than just sex. Stop this. 'You've just had too much to drink." He turned towards me, trying to get me to face him.

"I can't, Fox, I just can't let you in. I've been too hurt. It's not going to happen. I'm broken." I cried and faced him, tears rolling down my face as I searched his eyes desperate for an explanation as to why I was feeling so heartbroken.

"You know this is more than it is," he comforted me warmly, but I could see he was having a battle with himself internally. "Come here." He grabbed my face, wiping the tears and kissing me gently. I kissed him back like there was nothing more important in the world. I had started to fall in love already with the most unlikely personality on the planet and I had no idea what I was doing, or even what he was doing with me. "Go in and get some rest. I'll call you in the morning," he said softly. He kissed me once more, helped me out of the car and then reluctantly drove off into the distance. I staggered to my door but felt like I was being watched and turned around to look over my shoulder.

Kicking my muddy heels off, I looked in the mirror and noticed that my top was on inside out and the wrong way around. Lipstick was all over my face. I was a little shocked at my appearance, but then thought 'ah fuck it'. I'd just had the most incredible sex and he liked me. Flopping onto my bed, I knocked the cucumber onto the floor and burst out laughing!

Chapter Fifteen:
I Did it My Way

It had been a few weeks now since I moved into my new home and I'd heard about another opportunity for employment via a colleague. We had both decided to jump ship at the same time. He had handed his notice in a few days ago and I was going to do it tomorrow. Although I'd miss working with Fox to recruit his staff, it was probably completely unprofessional of me to be shagging the brains out of a client. I'd had a brief telephone interview and was seeing the lady CEO in a few days but felt confident I would get the job. It was a completely different direction for me and I was excited; it felt like this could be the right move for me.

Tucking myself into my cosy bed, I put some soothing music on, drank a glass of wine and texted the Fox to say goodnight, but had no notification of it being read, so figured he was asleep. His phone always goes onto airplane mode when he's got to be up early in the morning, much the same of a weekend when he's with his children.

I had the nightmare neighbour from hell who was making so much noise. "Shut the fuck up, Shrek," I shouted, and the sound settled down for a few minutes before it started again, even louder than before. God, he's like a poltergeist! 'Ping.' I picked up my wine glass and grabbed my phone from the side of the bed, hoping it was Fox, or maybe a priest!

'*Evening L.J., how are you?*' I looked at the message and bolted upright in bed, surprised, reluctant to reply. Well, if it's not long-lost Wanker Pants! '*Apart from my neighbour from HELL and being a little tipsy, I'm just fine.*' I sipped my wine and refilled the glass, waiting for his comeback. '*Ha, are you in bed?*' I shook my head, thanks for the concern dickhead, he still thought he owned me. '*I'm all tucked up in bed*' secretly frightened I might get murdered in my sleep. '*Had any new fantasies lately?*' he asked curiously. '*Oh, all the time. You?*' I lied, bored already; he never changed. I knew what was coming, but maybe this time I could play him at his own game.

'*Yeah, I've had a few.*' I picked up my phone and clicked onto some porn that I'd been watching, since anything was better than listening to next door, and I sent him the link. '*Here, watch this, it will get you to sleep.*' I clicked send and thought he might just fuck off and let me sleep. '*I like the amateur stuff, so that's hot. Anyway, it's time you came up with some new ideas.'* I typed away furiously at my comeback, my blood starting to boil. I hated the way he talked to me, I had not heard from him in months and he was demanding sex again. *'Well, you beat that, tell me what you want to do to me, that we have not ALREADY done.'* I knew he'd have nothing interesting to say after that, it always ended up the same, show me your pussy, put something in it, send it to me on video and then I'll mysteriously disappear.

'Okay... I want to tie you to four chairs in my kitchen, positioned on all fours, so you can't move, blind folded, with your bum in the air, so I can whip your ass hard with my jeans belt.' I sat up in bed shocked and a little aroused. *'So, I wouldn't be able to do anything? I'd be completely vulnerable, literally unable to move?'* I quizzed worriedly. *'Oh... and then I'd gag you, so you didn't talk shit and spoil the moment,'* he added directly, and I rolled my eyes. *'Then what would you do? I mean how are you supposed to fuck me, with the chairs in the way?'* I had visions of me boxed in and hadn't obviously quite grasped the concept clearly in my wine addled imagination. *'I'd be able to push them apart and do what the fuck I like to you.'* I frowned and started to worry slightly about the logistics of the situation.

'I take it you'd like to fuck me OR fuck me with an object then?' I asked yawning. This was dull. *'I'm going to fuck you with anything I can find and stick it*

up your asshole.' I pulled a funny face and messaged back. '*But that's such a delicate position to be in, doggie style always creates so much AIR, what if I did a massive fanny fart or even worse an actual fart, it would echo around your kitchen like someone emptying a can of baked beans, at deafening volume!!!*' I sent the text and sat back thinking that I'd just talked shit again and hopefully turned him completely off. '*Hahahaha… I'm crying,*' was his reply. It was always a surprise when I made him laugh; he was so pushy and grumpy usually.

'*Maybe a nice idea if you stuck a cork up my ass.*' I rolled my eyes and expected him to retire to bed. '*Like I said, it's about time you had some ideas L.J.*' he changed quickly back to his old cold self. '*Well, we've done most things, how about some dirty talk?*' I knew I couldn't do this unless it was in person, so I expected it to be over quickly. '*I'd walk into your house and slowly strip for you, not letting you take your eyes off me. I'd play with myself, turning you on, not letting you come near me, other than to suck my finger and taste me.*' I closed my eyes and started a seduction scene in my head and just decided to go with the flow. '*Mmmm, go on…*' he sent a blushing emoji.

'*Then I'd crawl towards you on all fours where you are sat in your living room and start to unbutton your fly, with you still dressed.*' An awful image of his shit slippers being there from last time entered my head and I tried to shake it from my thoughts. '*Keep going*,' he said, with one hand obviously up to no good. '*I'd then put your rock-hard cock in my mouth and suck, undressing your lower half slowly, pulling your trousers gradually to the floor and pushing them out of the way. Then I'd turn you around and make you go on all fours in front of me so I could lick your balls and your asshole and smack your ass hard.*' I was starting to get a bit flushed and quite assertive with him. '*Then what?*' he urged.

'*S*hut the fuck up, Fancy Pants, you're at my mercy now. Let me continue.*' I texted so fast, it just kept pouring out and I couldn't stop it, I wanted to put him in his place and show him what he had missed out on by dumping me. '*I'd let you feel how wet I was, rubbing my wet pussy all over you, pulling your hair and grabbing your cock with my hands, tossing you off, facing away from me.*'

'*Oh my GOD, L.J., this is naughty.*' He gave me a big thumbs up. I ignored him and continued. '*Then I'd squirt all over you, drenching you and making you cum at the same time, not even able to look at me, touch me, or kiss me.*'

'*Right, I'm off to bed,*' I said with conviction. Finally having more power than him was satisfying. I'd just outgrown Fancy Pants in the bedroom, and he damn well knew it. Was this because of the Silver

Fox? I'd never talk to Fox like that, I had too much respect. '*Night*,' he replied with a kiss. I raised my eyebrow, put my tongue out at the phone and blew a raspberry. What a jerk, I shouldn't have even answered your text, but I couldn't resist pissing you off. I set my alarm and put my phone on airplane mode so Icould get some peace, sank into my pillow and smiled until I fell fast asleep.

Chapter Sixteen:
The Best is Yet to Come

I parked up outside my office and tried not to be sick with nerves. I'd rehearsed my leaving speech over and over again in my head: "It's not the company or the shit hotels you put me up in, or the fact that you shout at me after every mistake," (It probably didn't help that I was shagging one of my clients and came into work hung over most days.) "but I just don't feel like it's right for me." My phone pinged and I quickly checked it before I left the car and took the walk of shame.

"Last night was fun. I forgot to ask you if you got the book published?" I was surprised that he had even remembered, it was so long ago that we had seen each other, and he had been a little drunk. I looked for a copy of my contract and attached it to a message to prove it was real.

"Wow, I'm impressed. I've never known an author before, well done," he said in shock. "Didn't think you'd ever really written a book to be honest. So, it's really about us fucking?" he continued, becoming nosey.

"Yeah, but your name isn't mentioned, don't worry. Like I said, I call you Mr. Fancy Pants." Wanker Pants, I thought to myself, knowing how much love I had put into the book, with no appreciation.

"It's out in the shops in two weeks," I continued, feeling smug. "You'll have to pick yourself a copy up, or I can send you one signed, if you like?" I thought to myself; I want you to, I hope you do, to see how much I loved you and how much you fucked me up and fucked me over. Maybe you will learn your lesson and not do this to anyone else ever again after that.

"We'll see. Got to go now; I'm at work. Busy day," and he was gone. What was the point in that conversation? It had literally got me nowhere, and now I was wound up and scared about handing my notice in, with another monster hangover. So, I decided to call Fox to calm me down.

"Fox, oh, thank god you answered," I said, rushing my words out. "I'm handing my notice in, like I told you I would if they didn't treat me better. On top of that Fancy Pants got back in contact last night, told me he wanted to tie me to four chairs and then texted me again today about the book. He's such a massive cockhead. He still thinks he owns me," I blurted out.

"Four chairs? That's a bit tame for him," he jested. "Look, just be calm, say what you need to say and leave. You know this other job looks promising. You will be fine; just be polite, no swearing and don't mention me," he said sternly.

"Fox, I need a good seeing to. I can't wait to see you later; it will one hundred percent de-stress me. I'll be in Cambridge at the publishers for four p.m. I'm driving down straight from here, then I will travel back up to stay with you in the hotel. I have a belated birthday surprise for you."

"Mmmm... what is it?" he asked in his usual deep sexy voice.

"A big red fucking bow wrapped around me, with stockings, suspenders and slutty heels to wrap around your head," I blurted out with excitement, not able to wait to surprise him.

"L.J., I've just pulled up outside the office, hard. You have to go. Good luck, I'll see you tonight."

I sat back in my car seat, took a deep breath, then opened my door, letting out my long legs, with power heels on.

"Morning, L.J.," my manager said without even looking up from his desk.

I walked towards him and waited for him to pay attention to me. "Can we have a quick chat, please. I think all the managers should come into the board room," I said quietly but assertively.

"Can't you see I'm busy?" he snapped. That disregard for my emotions was clear again; I had already told him I needed a meeting, so he'd had warning. God, I was surrounded by dickheads, they were everywhere: Fancy Pants, my boss... thank god my future manager would be a woman.

"I'm handing my notice in, boss," I said loudly so everyone could hear and walked into the board room leaving the door open and not sitting down. Jumping out of his seat dramatically he followed me, as did the other two and then we all sat down. I pushed my door key into the middle of the table. "I want to thank you all for the opportunity, but this just isn't working out. I don't feel like this is the right market for me; it's not making me happy. My hours are too long and, quite frankly, I don't appreciate being talked to like shit every day. I understand that I am the only female in the office, but I have asked you a few times now to talk to me better and warned you that I'd leave if things didn't change." I pushed my chair back, stood up tall and shook everyone's hands.

"I emailed my handover to you this morning. If you have any questions just call me. I take it you're quite happy for me to leave?" I tried not to start crying; I hated letting people down, but I was miserable working for the company.

"L.J., we think you're right. You're a nice girl, and we wish you all the best." I turned to one of the managers, who had always been kind to me, and he stood up and gave me a hug. "Good luck with the book L.J. I hope you become the next J.K. Rowling," he beamed. I looked at my boss, and his face was red with anger, but he contained himself and said goodbye. I thought about telling him that he needed to sort his fucking attitude problem out, but knew I needed a reference.

Walking out of the door I smelt the fresh air and bolted to my car, with a mixture of feelings. Where was I getting this strength from? I didn't have to put up with people being mean or talking down to me; I was going to go somewhere in life. Filled with excitement and nerves I set off on the long journey to meet my publisher.

Chapter Seventeen:
Born Free

Driving to Cambridge was a feat in itself. I got lost on several occasions but had set off in good time to allow for my lack of navigational skills. I arrived in a business park, asked for directions and finally found Pegasus. Looking in my car mirror, I gave myself a pep talk, put some lipstick on, grabbed my suit jacket and got out of the car. I approached the door and walked in, facing a wall in front of me that, from floor to ceiling, had rows upon rows of books. I gasped and pressed the bell in reception, starting to feel nervous. A very smart lady approached me and I reached out to shake her hand. "Hi, I'm L.J. Brown, author of A Year of Tiramisu." I smiled widely and she acknowledged who I was immediately, asking me to take a seat and telling me that the team would be with me shortly.

I waited for a good five minutes before two quite young women approached me and shook my hand, directing me to the meeting room. "Hello, L.J., it's great to finally meet you. Can I get you a coffee? Tea? Water?" I thought to myself secretly, wine would be great right now. I was a total bag of nervous energy and worried I would screw this up. I followed them into a large meeting room with a massive meeting table that could have easily fitted twenty people. The table had books stacked on it, along with water, and paper and pens to make notes.

"Thank you for coming today, L.J. We always like to meet our authors and we loved your book. I'm from publicity. We became so excited when we received your book." She beamed at me and waited for my response. I think slightly surprised that I didn't look like a hooker. I was dressed very smartly in a matching black business suit.

"Thank you for taking the time to meet with me. I'm sorry, I'm a little bit overwhelmed by all of it if I'm honest. I didn't even expect to become a writer let alone be published, it's just something that kind of happened to me." I was speaking way too fast, just like the day I did the presentation for Fox. I had stage fright.

"We read it and thought Oh my god, what is she going to get up to next? It's so gripping we couldn't put it down." Giggling, she seemed quite impressed and delighted about the book and its possibilities.

"Well, the book kind of fell out of me: it was like I'd been taken over by something. The sex is hot, right? I mean, I know people write about sex all the time." I rushed my words out anxiously, blushing slightly.

"Yes of course it's very hot, we loved it. Fifty Shades was BDSM — this is completely different. It's got a new angle; it has a completely different approach to sex. You have quite the imagination L.J.," she said, impressed.

"Oh, it's not my imagination; it's all true. That's why it was easy to write." I looked at them and two mouths fell open slightly. "Although some of it is a slight exaggeration," I continued, trying to save them from thinking I was a completely crazy nympho.

"Does Mr. Fancy Pants know about the book?" they questioned, dying to know the answer like it was a good bit of gossip.

"Yes, I think it's given him rather a large head. He's read bits of it and just laughed about it; he doesn't care about anything or anyone but himself, so he's cool with the book. It doesn't mention his name anyway." I looked down at my fingers and felt upset slightly, knowing all my hard work had been for nothing.

"Oh, absolutely, he's an awful man," they said at the same time. I looked shocked and then admitted to myself that they were right and that I shouldn't be surprised.

"He's absolutely not Mr Right," I continued, not wanting to say the words out loud, but the truth was now burning into me like a hot iron and guilt hit me every time I mentioned his name.

"He's definitely not your Mr Right. No happy ending there, I'm afraid," the lady from publicity said firmly.

"I don't think anyone has written about the online dating world and it's dangers either. I think this is the book's USP?" They agreed and continued to listen; I think they could tell I was very nervous. "So, what happens next?" I changed the subject and focused.

"We will edit it. Once it's edited, we will then send it to you for review. After you've approved it, we will put it into paperback and then start to advertise it on the web. We will contact newspapers, radio stations and everything we can think of to get the book out there!" she said with conviction and confidence that it would sell. "We will contact Amazon, Waterstones, Barnes and Noble, all the largest bookshops, and ask them if we can sell the book with them; then it usually just grows from there." I looked at them wide eyed.

"Waterstones would be a dream come true." I began to feel emotional and tears started to well up in my eyes.

"So, you think it has massive potential?" I asked excitedly.

"We can't give any guarantees. But sex sells, and you do have something unique. We definitely think you need to go with the 'based on a true story' theme; it will get more readers interested. We think this and the sequel will hopefully do very well." They looked at me excitedly. "Do you have any other questions for us?" I looked at them, shell shocked. The fact that I was an author had finally hit me and I was already thinking about the next book and how I could talk about the Silver Fox and everything we'd been getting up to.

"No." I shook my head barely able to speak because I was so choked with emotion.

"One of my friends read the book. She's an English teacher and she said she'd written dissertations longer and that one of her GCSE students could write a better piece of work. She said she would fully support me if I wanted to become a prostitute, but this book was just awful." I blurted it out without thinking and they looked back at me with complete surprise. "I have no filter. I'm sorry, if I feel something then I usually just say it." I blushed and started to pack away my notes.

"Has she written a book, L.J?" the lady from publishing asked me.

"Not that I know of," I replied.

"There's your answer, right there. I don't think she's much of a friend, dear," she said comforting me.

"L.J., it's been a pleasure to meet you. We are really looking forward to working with you. Here are our business cards, please email if you have any questions. Let's do this!" The room was full of positivity again. I was excited to be a part of this amazing journey. Wow, I was officially an author! It was real!

I got into my car and the first call I made was to the Fox. He answered immediately. "L.J., are you okay?"

"Oh my god, Fox, I'm more than okay!" I screamed down the phone with so much energy and excitement, and we went into deep conversation about what happened in the meeting. I don't think I'd ever been so high or felt so free before in my life. "You are so going to get some amazing fucking sex tonight!"

Chapter Eighteen:
Jeepers Creepers

I don't know how I got to the hotel. I was on speakerphone to the Fox most of the way, and in a world of my own for the rest of the time. Pulling up I raised an eyebrow; it was an impressive spa hotel. "Always the best for Fox," I snorted to myself in amusement. I couldn't even afford a bed and breakfast, and at this rate if I didn't get a job offer soon, I'd be living in a cardboard box. He had called to say he was running late and to sign in and go to the room, order anything I needed and wait for him. I'd already picked up a few bottles of red for us and was looking forward to celebrating and sleeping overnight. It was rare we ever got chance to spend the night together, with our busy lives and living so far away from each other.

The hotel room was unbelievable; I gasped in amazement. It had a massive oak bed stacked with pillows and a beautiful state of the art bathroom. Mirrors were everywhere, so I knew exactly why he'd picked it. I placed my case by the window and looked out at the view. We even had our own hot tub;

it was perfect. I searched inside my bag, got my phone and decided to call him, opening the first bottle of wine and pouring some into a glass I had found in the bathroom.

"Fox, you sexy fucker, where are you?" I sipped my wine and glided around the hotel room gracefully spinning around, inspecting everything and getting ideas in my head of what I could get up to in it.

"I'm stuck in traffic; it looks like I'm going to be at least another hour." He sounded stressed and tired.

"Well, guess what I'm doing," I giggled down the phone.

"Drinking wine," he replied quickly.

"Apart from that," I hissed playfully.

"Go on, tease me." He sounded sexy now and more relaxed.

"I'm on our bed, completely naked, having a little play." I paused and waited.

"How are you playing?" He took a deep breath.

"I've got my fingers inside me, then I'm slowly rubbing my wet clit, thinking of you licking it." I put my fingers in my mouth and sucked them, letting him hear, then moaned down the phone.

"I'm putting my foot down; I'll be there asap. Stay where you are." And he hung up the phone.

Jumping into the shower, I sang at the top of my voice, dancing around, thinking about my day and how amazing it had been already. Not to mention I was about to be in the arms of someone I really liked for a fucking amazing shagathon.

"I'm an author; I'm an author; I'm an author!" I screamed until I could really hear it. Just like another time in the shower, when I had had to get used to the idea that I was really single and make it stick in my mind. It was like having some kind of strange déjà vu. That crazy little dream about a naughty book had become a reality. God, I've just really achieved something quite fucking cool.

My phone rang again, so I got out of the shower and reached for a towel. This time it was the lady CEO I had spoken to regarding the new job I had applied for. "Hi L.J. Thanks for speaking to me a few days ago. Can we arrange the interview for Friday this week at ten a.m.?"

"Yes, that would be fantastic. Thank you for getting back to me so quickly." I smiled down the phone and bounced around the room quietly. Could this day get any better, I thought to myself. I feel like I've won the lottery. We talked about the company and the role in a bit more depth and I drank some more wine, starting to feel a bit lightheaded and also cold from being wrapped in a towel for so long. Finishing the conversation, I dashed to the bathroom with my case and pulled out a matching bra and panties in black lace with a tiny hint of pink. I sprayed my body with expensive perfume and began to dry my long dark hair, looking in the mirror at myself and starting to feel sexy.

Looking at my body in the mirror, I followed my curves. My breasts were pert and my nipples soft and pink; my stomach was flat and smooth, and my pussy was perfectly shaven, and now looking amazing with a black lace thong hanging on my hips. My face was flushed from the wine; my deep blue eyes glared at me in the mirror, turned on by the situation, hungry for what was going to happen. I put a light coating of blush on my cheeks and worked on my eyes. Black around my eyelashes and all the way round to define them, followed by mascara and white liner to make my eyes stand out more with my thick dark eyebrows. I took a swig of wine and applied thick red lipstick and blotted it several times so it would stay on.

Leaning away from the mirror I examined myself and tended to my hair, creating volume and spraying it with perfume. Bending over I shook it and sprayed it lightly with hairspray making it neat again. "Perfect," I said to myself, pushing my breasts together and giving myself a little wink. Laughing and starting to dance around the bedroom, I looked in my case for the most important part of the outfit, and pulled out a red bow. Working out how to wear it had me falling over a few times, but I finally stepped into it and it was on. It looked amazing, deep red and shiny over my breasts and across my body. The final touch was my killer black stiletto heels. I looked in the mirror once more and gasped. I slipped a few bangles around my arm, put on some nice earrings and I was done. All I had to do now was wait on the bed looking sexy and drinking wine.

"God, you're in for a treat tonight Mr. I'm feeling very fucking horny and sexy.," I said to myself out loud. I was spinning around the room dancing to songs playing on YouTube on my phone, when it rang again.

"I'm here, L.J. I'm just grabbing some food to bring to the room, I've not had anything to eat all day." He sounded abrupt and hung up again. He wants to sit and eat first, why had that instantly made me feel less important? I felt on guard and my good mood was disappearing fast. The door was open for him to come in and fifteen minutes later he rushed through with his bags and a plate of food. Putting it down he stood and just looked at me on the bed. "Oh my god, L.J., you look absolutely amazing." He rushed over to me, kissed me hard and pulled away to look again. "Wow...look at you... I'm so sorry, I'm going to have to get undressed and eat at the same time or I'm going to pass out from starvation," he apologised.

"Well, happy belated birthday, Fox. Do you like the bow?" I blushed, standing up and walking towards him, spinning around trying to dazzle him. Touching his face with my hand, I looked into his eyes and kissed him gently, getting some of his food stuck on my lips. We both laughed and he rushed to get undressed throwing some tablets on the table. "What are those?" I asked, looking worried.

"Viagra. I treated myself for my birthday. I want to stay inside you all night long." He glanced at me devilishly, pulling his tie over his head and trying to eat, getting tangled up and confused. I kissed him again, not taking my eyes off him and helped him get his trousers off and his pants down. He was hard as a rock and the desire in both our eyes was out of control. I pulled away and let him eat and take a tablet, kneeling on the edge of the bed I took off my bangles and threw them across the room trying to get them over his massive cock.

"Missed!" He laughed at me for my effort.

"Not that time," I giggled and fell back onto the bed in amusement, laughing. He then pounced from one side of the room to the bed and threw himself on top of me, crushing the red bow.

"Congratulations by the way, I'm proud of you. Here's your reward." He smirked, kissed me again and he was inside me.

"Oh, Fox, is that the Viagra?" I was surprised at how full I felt.

"No, that's just you, turning me on. The Viagra takes time to work." He smiled and kissed me again, ripping my bow off along with the rest of my clothes, but keeping my heels on. Pushing my legs apart, he went down on me, sticking his fingers inside me and licking me, watching me moan and throw myself about the bed. He then pulled me off the bed and made me stand up next to him. Walking and kissing, like people with two left feet, we moved to the bathroom and stood in front of the mirrors.

"Stay there; don't move." He left the room and I was left with my refection. My face was flushed, my hair all over the place and not much red lipstick left on, but I still felt sexy.

"Bend over the bath," he said gently, pushing me forward. Slowly he poured oil onto my ass so I could feel it trickle down into my pussy. I looked at him in the mirror and commented on him flushing; the tablets were starting to work for him. Slowly he eased himself into my ass and looked in the mirror as he was doing it, making me face the mirror so I could look into his eyes. The oil was still on his hands and he grabbed my breasts, squeezing them hard, rubbing them with oil and holding them tight while he thrust into me. "I'm going to take your ass, hard," he whispered in my ear. I gulped and nodded in agreement; we hadn't fucked hard this way yet, but it was something we both wanted to experience because we had discussed it several times.

Slowly at first, he pushed deep inside me, taking my breath away. It hurt a little, but still felt good. Then fast and hard, over and over until I was blissful, and I was starting to build. "Fuck me harder, Fox!" I screamed, watching him in the mirror. We were both becoming aggressive, like animals. I was literally being ruined by him.

"Fuck L.J.," he screamed out, "this is so good!"

"Shut up… Just fuck me, Fox." I smacked my hands down onto the bath and bent right over so he could go even deeper inside me.

"L.J. Oh. God! No! Fuck!" he cried out.

"Put it back in. What are you doing?" I pulled my head back up to look at him in the mirror. To my absolute horror there was blood all up my back and all over him. I shot upright and looked at him worried and speechless.

"I've torn my cock," he yelped, blood pouring from him. It was the deepest red blood I had ever seen, and his cock was instantly starting to swell.

"Oh my god, I'm sorry. What do we do? Get it under a cold tap?" I moved him across to the sink holding his bloody cock and turning on the water. It washed away the blood, but it kept coming.

"We've just been too rough, that's all. It will stop," he said in pain and shock.

"Have you done this before?" I questioned him.

"No one's ever asked me to fuck them that hard, so no!" He smirked at me, but then looked helpless and a little awkward as he tried wipe blood off me. I ran to get my phone to google what to do.

"Siri, tell me what to do when a man tears his penis." I rushed the words out, desperate to know how to stop him from bleeding.

"I'm sorry, I don't understand the question," it replied, making us both laugh out loud.

I sat on the edge of the bath cleaning myself off and reading to him what I had found on google. "Between the foreskin and shaft of your penis is the banjo string. If it's too tight, it can tear, usually during sexual intercourse." I rolled my eyes.

"No shit, Sherlock!" he said in pain.

"The bleeding usually stops without assistance, but if it keeps happening you must visit your GP or local hospital for advice," I continued, raising my eyebrow and smirking at him, before I got to the best bit; "You are advised not to have sex for six weeks after the tear happens," I gasped in shock and he looked shattered by the information I had given him.

"Six fucking weeks, we will both die," I said to him defeated.

"It's stopped bleeding, L.J." I turned to him and kissed his lips gently, worrying about him being in pain.

"I was only kidding; I made the six weeks part up," I gasped and covered my face with my hands. He chased me across the room, and I screamed with laughter when he caught me.

"L.J., you know there are lots of other things we can do until my penis recovers." My eyes lit up with excitement, I bit my lip and we sank back into bed, pulling the covers over our heads.

"I could bandage it up for you, Fox. I like playing doctors and nurses," I made reference to my book and he shut me up by passionately kissing me, until we were once again completely helpless in each other's arms.

"Shut the fuck up and do as you are told." He said into my mouth; eyes wide and wild and we were once again lost in another night of passion.

Chapter Nineteen:
It's Only a Paper Moon

A month had gone by, I'd been offered and started my new role and soon realised I had found my true passion, my dream job. Working with people who actually cared and wanted to help, was much better than working in sales. I was stressed out though; as well as training and working full time and being the mother of two children, I felt like I was under so much pressure to do the final edit of my book. The publishers had been sending me amendments and asking me questions about the flow of the book and things I had repeated or missed. I had never had to work so hard in my life, but it was finally finished and ready to go to print.

I parked up at the supermarket on a sunny day in late July. My kids were fighting, and I had had enough of the summer holidays already. It felt like I was working for nothing, as all my money was going on childcare, and I had very little support from my ex-husband. I felt like I was going insane from the pressure and stress of everything that was happening to me and my weekends were taken up with extra work, to make sure I would do well in my job, and I tried to see the Fox whenever we got an opportunity. I literally never stopped working and was feeling ill and fragile. As I mindlessly pushed my trolley around the supermarket, my phone rang in my pocket and I answered it.

"Sis!" my sister screamed down the phone at me, "I'm with my friend Michelle; she just bought a copy of your book!" I promptly stopped walking down a shopping aisle where I was filling my trolley full of savers food.

"It can't be; my publisher hasn't told me that it's out yet," I said down the phone in surprise.

"Well, it is! I'll put you on to her."

An excited friend of my sister' began to talk to me. "It's true; I have it in my hand. I ordered it a few days ago on Amazon. Will you sign it for me? I loved it!" I froze to the spot in shock.

"Really? You have it? Oh my god!" I started to jump up and down on the spot with excitement in the middle of the supermarket not even caring if people were looking at me. "Of course, I will. Thank you so much for buying it." I beamed at everyone walking past me.

"I'll put you back on to your sister. 'You're really talented, well done. It is so funny and so heart-warming. I can't wait for the next one to come out," she said with love and I knew she'd understood it. I was so overwhelmed I didn't know what to say other than 'thank you'.

"Sis, Oh my god it's real!" I screamed down the phone at her.

"You did it, Kiddo. You're an author!" I heard her sweet loving voice and started to cry, unable to contain myself. My daughter was beside me and asked me what was wrong, and I just said I had had some good news.

"It's happened... I feel sick... Holy, fudge!" People looked at me and I lowered my head trying to contain my excitement and surprise. "Have you told Mum and Dad?" I asked her, my head racing and my heart pounding.

"I left them both voicemails," she said excitedly. "No turning back now, Sis... I love you!"

"I love you too! Sis, what if people hate it?" I looked at the wine selection and grabbed the cheapest bottle, just so I could cope with what had just happened.

"Where are you, Sis?" she asked, "Why don't you come over to celebrate?" she beamed down the phone.

"I'm in Aldi, buying bargain toilet roll and shit food; I've got no money for petrol to get to you, or I would."

"I'll lend you some. Come up and see us." She didn't sound shocked, as she'd heard it so many times before.

"No, it's fine, honestly. I have the kids and I'm in shock. I will come up when I have some money." I didn't want to ask for help again. "I will see you soon, I promise. I love you so much." and I rang off, and paid for my things at the checkout. Flying high, I pushed the trolley out of the supermarket and packed my things into the car. The kids were fighting, but I didn't seem to care. I was in a bubble… a bubble of wonderfulness.

I sat in the front of the car and got my phone out to text the Fox. I brought up WhatsApp and sent him the link to Amazon with my book details for purchase, with the text, *IT'S OUT* and a million love hearts. Sitting back in my seat, I turned on the engine and put the radio at full blast, only to hear 'Starving' playing, which had been mine and fancy pants song. My heart sank, and I looked up to the sky and shook my head; this moment belonged to me it, was not for him! Changing the channel to BBC Radio Leeds, I set off, putting my shades on, singing at the top of my voice and not giving a care in the world.

Chapter Twenty:
Something Stupid Like I Love You...

Weeks had gone by and the book was all over the internet, in every corner of the world. My dream had come true; it was in Waterstones. America was starting to notice it and I was permanently in shock. Every day I woke up, another bookstore or website was selling it and reviews were coming in thick and fast. The L.J. Brown Facebook page had thousands of followers, and I knew that people were loving reading the truth about sex and online dating. Women all around the world were messaging me to say they had had the same things happen to them and were amazed I'd dared to write about it.

Men love it. I had hit the opposite market from Fifty Shades. Bored housewives were not reading it. Men, players and those stuck in shit relationships or marriages, were relating to it. A few of the male fans became a little overwhelming at times and pretty much all of them wanted to shag me, so eventually, after discussing it at length with the publisher, I shut my fan mail down and just posted funny teasers.

Nasty reviews were coming in as well as good reviews. I was convinced that Fancy Pants was responsible for many of the bitter comments that had been written, calling me a prostitute.

Turning my light off, I decided to get an early night, as I had to take the kids to their dads for the weekend in the morning. I texted Fox goodnight and told him I missed him, then started to fall asleep when my phone began to ring. Not even looking at who it was, because I knew it would be Fox, I answered. "It's too late for phone sex!" I moaned softly down the phone.

"Ewww... L.J., that's gross!" My friend Jemma snorted down the phone. Jumping up in bed and putting my light back on, I was startled and apologised, laughing at the mistake.

"Sorry, I was expecting it to be someone else," I rubbed my eyes and fell back on the pillow.

"Are you seeing Fancy Pants again?" She sounded frustrated. "You know he's just using you? I have no idea why you even bother with the loser." I could hear her struggling with cooking something.

"What time is it?" I asked, rubbing my eyes again and yawning.

"It's eight thirty. Are you in bed? It's not like you; are you okay?"

"I'm fine. I'm just working so hard and this book is taking over my life." I picked a copy up off my bedside table and smiled, throwing it back down. "So, you haven't seen him? Really? Are you telling me the truth?" I rolled my eyes and told her I'd met someone new. "Why do I not know about this?" She stopped what she was doing and paid full attention. "So, you're over Fancy Pants?"

"Yeah, I guess so. I've not told you because I wasn't sure, I am now." I smiled widely in acknowledgement that I knew I had made my mind up, finally.

"Is the sex good? What's he like? What does he do? Where did you meet?" she threw a million questions at me. "You didn't meet on a dating site, did you?"

"No, nothing like that. It was a pure accidental fate thing, I guess." I thought back to the presentation and looking into Fox's eyes for the first time.

"L.J., you sound different. I can't believe it; are you in love?"

"I don't know really; how do you know?" I thought I'd been in love before, but I hadn't been. I struggled with myself trying to work it all out.

"Well, does he make you feel like you're excited and desperate to see him? Like you're floating on air, like Fancy Pants did? I've read your book; I know you were crazy about him."

"Well, it's completely different..." I started to daydream; there were so many things that were different, so many new feelings.

"How? What's the difference? It's got to be better than Fancy Pants. God, that guy is vomit on a pile of shit!" I laughed and thought to myself about how I truly felt about the Fox.

"When I'm with him, I'm completely myself. I'm happy and secure. It's the most natural thing in the world. Time just seems to stop; it's like magic. When I'm not with him, I know I will see him again, I don't need to worry about the next time. I just look forward to it. I've never felt this before with anyone and I've been fighting it for a few months, but I can't anymore; it's taken over me." I felt a glow with the thought of him and tried to snap out of it.

"L.J., are you in love? Finally settling for someone?" She sounded shocked and disbelieving.

"Yeah, I think I fucking am." Sitting up in bed playing with my hair, I stared into space. I felt so peaceful, grinning down the phone.

"Does this mean you're going to fuck Fancy Pants off, once and for all? We all need you to! The world has started a hate campaign against him; have you seen your reviews?" She seemed pleased with the fact that it was not just her that hated him.

"I'll never go near that vile man again," I said assertively and knew that it was completely over, and that my heart no longer needed or wanted him.

"L.J., this is brilliant! When are you going to let me meet him? I don't even know his name," excited for me, she became pushy.

"Oh, no, not yet... We are going to take it slow. Only fools rush in and all that." I knew we had talked about keeping this quiet until we were ready.

"Does he have a big cock?" she laughed down the phone.

"Well, it's bigger than I'm used to for sure," I burst into laughter and went downstairs to get a drink.

"L.J., have you seen how mental your book's going? It's sold out everywhere; when are we going to celebrate?" She sounded excited for me that everything was fitting into place.

"I'm free this weekend. How about we do it after I drop the kids off? I can come to you. I could do with a break." I jumped up and down on the spot, trying to keep warm.

"Okay. Well Miss 'I'm in love, new, up-and-coming Author', I'll see you tomorrow and we can get totally pissed!" With a crash of pans and a lot of swearing, she hung up. Dragging myself up the stairs, I tucked myself into bed and turned out the lights, ALL of them. For the first time in my life, I was no longer scared of the dark. Holding my pillow, I smiled and fell into a deep peaceful sleep.

Chapter Twenty-one:
Please Be Kind

"Mummy, can I come in for cuddles?" My little boy jumped onto my bed and wrapped himself around me tightly.

"Good morning, sweetheart, did you sleep well?" I gave him a kiss on his forehead.

"I had bad dreams," he looked at me with a scared face.

"What did you dream about darling?" I asked sympathetically, giving him my full attention.

"I dreamt that the man across the road chased me down the street then ate me." His bottom lip quivered, and he put on his super sad face. "I don't like this house mummy; can we move again?" I looked up at the ceiling and thought of ways I could get out of my contract.

"I promise," I said to him comfortingly, "as soon as I get some commission from my new job, I will find us a beautiful house, away from him."

"He scares me mummy." He started to cry, so I wrapped him in a blanket and started to sing to him, and then tickled him, to get him back into a good mood.

"Well, it's your weekend at dad's, so shall we get ready to go?" I looked at him excitedly. Jumping out of bed, we went down for breakfast and started to get ready. We heard banging and screaming outside, so I got my iPhone headphones and put them in his ears and plugged it into my phone on YouTube, so he didn't have to hear it.

"Mummy your phone's ringing!" I walked back into the living room, saw that it was my brother and answered it.

"Hi Bro, you okay?" I said, holding the phone to my ear while trying to cook breakfast and iron clothes, all at the same time.

"You called me," he said coldly.

"I didn't. Oh, sorry, maybe my boy's been pressing buttons.". I poured a coffee and looked out into my back garden.

"You are making a fool out of yourself. Your book's nothing new, L.J.; it's not going to make you any money." He had never spoken to me like this before and he seemed serious.

"Is this because you lent me money to get it published? I've told you I will pay you back. You don't need to worry about that. Besides, that's what families do. I'd have helped you, if the boot was on the other foot."

"L.J., if it was any good you wouldn't have had to pay anything; they would have just signed you. You're just like everyone else that wants to be a writer. 'It's easy to get a book published; you can even self-publish." He sounded bored.

"Have you ever had a dream? It will sell and I will do well. These things take time," I said deflated. "Can't you just be happy and proud that I have done this?" I started to get cross and tears welled up in my eyes. The walls were shaking with banging outside; my little boy ran up to me and hid behind my legs, almost knocking me over.

"Look, L.J., I wish you all the best, but if you don't pay me my money back like we arranged, I will send the bailiffs round to collect it. I hope that is very clear to you," he said with venom.

"I actually can't believe you just said that to me. I'm your sister. What the hell has got into you? I don't remember you ever being this way before, are you pissed? Have you even read it?" I questioned him.

"My wife has. We have decided that we don't talk about your book in our house," he snapped.

"What the hell is that supposed to mean?" I couldn't process all the information, I was overwhelmed and hurt.

"Mummy, Mummy… I don't like it. I want to go to Daddy's." My little boy began to cry because of the neighbours.

"Look, just make sure you pay me the money back and I wish you luck, but you're being completely unrealistic. It's a pipe dream and it won't make you money." He then hung up.

I came from a broken home, my mum and dad separated just after I turned one and I didn't know my dad and my half-brother properly until a few years previously. The marriage had ended because my dad had had an affair with my mother's best friend, so there were a lot of very bitter feelings and anger towards him. I was brought up by my mother, and from the age of three, a stepfather who didn't like children lived with us. I never remember having a loving male role model, this had probably made my search for love so much harder.

Dashing out of the house with my overnight bag, I got the children into the car and set off to their dad's. I couldn't get away from the house fast enough. My phone rang in the car and so I connected to the speaker phone and answered; it was the Fox.

"Morning, young lady, it's a beautiful day," and he did as he usually did and started to sing to me.

"Hey Fox," I said in a fragile voice.

"What's wrong? Are you okay? Are the kids okay?" he asked, worried.

"My brother just told me he thinks the book's not going to have any impact, that everything's been written about already, and I'm being unrealistic." I rush my words, welling up and fighting the tears. "Then he said he'd send the bailiffs round to my house, if I didn't pay him back," I blurted out panicked.

"Okay, calm down. Take a deep breath and look at it logically, not emotionally." He was trying to stop me spiralling out of control with my emotions.

"Everyone is entitled to their opinion. He might be right, but then again, he might be wrong. You don't know what's going on in his life at the moment; he might not be in a great place himself." I had not thought of that. "Have you borrowed from him before?"

I felt sick with worry about telling the truth. "Yes, to move to a new house. My dad helped too." I thought Fox might go mad because I was financially unstable.

"Did you pay him back?" he lowered his tone and paused.

"No, not yet, but I plan to. I've been getting back on my feet, it's only been a few months since I moved." I felt like I was making excuses.

"Little tip for the future: never borrow money from family or friends. Try to not borrow at all, then you will never have this situation again." He was always full of wise advice and I fell silent, deep in thought.

"I've looked on the web. Your book's everywhere. How cool does that feel?" he said, trying to make me feel happy.

"I guess it's pretty cool. Where are you anyway? What are you doing today?" I wished I could be with him; I needed a hug.

"I'm packing, ready for Germany next week. Big conference to attend," he said smiling down the phone.

"I wish I could come," I said softly to him, trying to not push things too far; we'd never had a few days together, let alone a week away.

"What are you up to, isn't it your weekend off?" He seemed more interested in my life than his.

"I'm meeting up with Jemma and Mr Star Wars. I've got them both signed copies; I promised I would once it was out, so we are off for a few drinks." I started to brighten up a bit and shook off the abuse from my brother.

"Have you got yourself a blow-up doll for the hotel room?" I laughed down the phone at him, knowing he would be surrounded by men all week, trying to lighten the mood.

"I think the room comes with a real feel doll. If not, I will get one on room service." We both laughed and then I instantly missed him again. "My phone will be off tonight as I'll be in the air, just so you know if you can't reach me. I will need to sort out the Wi-Fi in my room so we can facetime." He instantly made me feel at ease, not having to worry about other women being in his bed, which is where my head had already started to lead me. "Take care, young lady, have a good night with your friends and I will catch up with you tomorrow." He paused for a few seconds, waiting for me to say goodbye or express my feelings.

"When I'm rich and famous, I'm going to hire a plane and that 'I don't give a fuck' fantasy will become a reality," I grinned wickedly and stopped at the traffic lights.

"And there she is; L.J. is back. As long as you don't turn into a strawberry, then I'm in," he said with confidence. "You will be fine. Don't listen to anyone and keep thinking positively. If you put yourself out there in the public eye, you're going to get some shit back. If you tell people you're doing well, they will try to put you down. If you're doing shit some people will have your back and try to help, but the majority of people don't even care. Right, I really have to leave, my ride is here to the airport. Speak to you later, L.J.," he said lovingly and hung up before I could say goodbye.

Arriving at my ex-husband's, he invited me in for the first time in months and offered me a coffee. I looked at him worried that he was going to tell me bad news; we never talked anymore. "So, I have a girlfriend," he blurted out.

"Oh, that's good. It's not the skank from down the road, with no teeth is it?" I jested and he look embarrassed.

"No, she's someone I've known for a long time, but it's just all kind of happened fast." He looked at me and for the first time in ages he looked happy and well. "You have that Fancy Pants from up the road, don't you still?" He looked uninterested.

"No, that's over. We were just shagging; he was never my boyfriend."

"Yeah, we were doing it wrong in bed, weren't we?" He looked at me and covered his face with his hands. "It was shit, our sex life. We were definitely doing it wrong." I nodded in agreement and we both burst out laughing.

"Why were we even together in the first place?" I said rolling my eyes. "We got our beautiful kids out of it; that's the main thing, but we are not compatible at all in that department." I grabbed his hand and kissed it. "This is a good thing. It means we can be good friends now, no more fighting. Let's just do this for our children and move on. And sort your fucking house out; it's a mess. I hope she can clean."

"Is your book out yet?" he asked, trying to change the subject.

"Yes, it's out. I'm going on the radio next week, BBC Radio Leeds. It's all taken me by surprise. I'm trying to stay level-headed though; it might never make me anything."

"Be nice if it does though; you can buy me a new carpet," he gently punched me on the shoulder playfully. My phone interrupted us, as it rang in my pocket.

"L.J., where's my signed book? I have champagne waiting on ice!" It was Mr. Star Wars.

"I'll be there in ten. Jemma's meeting me at yours; is that okay?" I began pacing around the room, getting excited.

"Yeah, that's fine. I'll see you soon, Obi Wan Kenobi." I grinned down the phone at him, then caught my ex-husband staring at me like I was a child.

"Got to dash; thank you for the coffee. Oh, and I wouldn't read the book. I was quite mad at you for shagging the godparent of our children. I called you a few choice words in the book; (never mentioned your name) but sorry anyway," leaving him with his mouth wide open, I dashed out of the house.

Chapter Twenty-two:
Blues in the Night...

I pulled up outside the local shop that I had once used all the time; it felt strange being back in it still seeing all the same faces. I grabbed two bottles of red wine and some nibbles. "Hello stranger, I've not seen you in over twelve months. Are you well? Your ex tells me you have a book coming out?" I looked at her shocked.

"Hey, it's nice to see you too. Yes, I have and thank you." I tried to get away as quickly as I could.

"So, what's it about then?" she continued, wanting gossip.

"It's a horror story. An ex-wife gets revenge on her lover, stalks him down and then kills him," I said coldly, ready to kill my ex for telling everyone. "Its nice to see you again!" I winked and left the shop.

For fuck's sake, how many people has he told, the stupid knob-head? Cursing I got back into my car and parked up outside my friend's house, grabbing my case, and proceeded to his door.

I pressed the buzzer and discovered that a Star Wars ring tone had been added. I laughed and pressed another six times. When he answered the door, I pretended to have a lightsabre. "Luke, I am your father. Mwahahaha." I grabbed him and gave him a big kiss and a hug. "That's a cool doorbell. Where did you get it? I want one," I smiled widely and handed him the wine and my jacket.

"L.J., you look great, Miss Author. How do you feel?" I reached inside my bag and pulled out a copy of the book I had signed earlier for him. We both flopped down onto the sofa and I handed him the book, he looked back at me and smiled. "You did it; how cool is this!" He reached over to hug me. I had written a personal message inside and signed it; I could tell it had touched him.

"The naughtiest, silliest little book on the shelves of Waterstones," I added and had a little jazz hands moment. "Our chapter is number fourteen. Flick to it and read it out loud." I rested my head on the sofa arm and watched him read, then got up to pour some wine for us both, still listening and laughing at his impression of me.

The doorbell rang again, and I got up to answer it. "It will be Jemma," I yelped with excitement.

"Is some famous author having a party!?" she held her hands out and grabbed me. We both screamed and she walked in with me and I introduced her to Mr Star Wars.

"Nice to meet you, Mr Star Wars. I've heard all about you and now so has the rest of the world, through her book." Laughing I asked her what she wanted to drink, and we all sat down with the books and flicked through.

I'd only had a few sips of wine as I wanted to pace myself and I needed to get ready to go out, so I left them both together chatting. It was a warm day and the patio windows overlooked the water front. They had both disappeared outside while I went to get changed and I could hear them chatting away. I had laid all my clothes on his bed and opened the window to let air in, I sat on the edge of the bed in my towel and logged onto Facebook. Sitting listening to them getting on so well was lovely for me; two of my best friends together.

"So, what do you really think about L.J?" I heard Jemma say and sat up getting closer to the window to listen. "I think this book has gone to her head," she said nastily. Shocked, I froze to the spot, she was being mean and out of order. I looked out of the window waiting for him to respond to her.

"Well, she can be a bit out there sometimes."

Sinking to the floor, I put my head in between my knees. My hair was dripping wet down my legs and tears began to flow.

Picking up my phone, I was about to post something about friendship on Facebook, and then leave, when I got a notification. It was Fancy Pants changing his relationship status to 'in a relationship'.' I scrolled down and clicked on his photo and there he was, looking like Aladdin with a deep tan and white shirt, with his arm around a brunette with a bigger nose than Concorde. I logged into snap chat and messaged him. *You're in a relationship? When did you ever decide that you wanted to settle down? Congratulations, but I'm in shock.* I question him without even thinking about what I was doing, and he replied almost immediately. *Thank you. I never said I didn't want a relationship*, he replied bluntly. *But your actions, you just liked fucking about.* I sounded desperate for answers. *But the book?* I continued. *I won't be buying a copy and I am really not interested L.J.* Before I could type my reply, I was blocked off everything.

"What is it with today!" I bolted up, grabbing my jeans and quickly getting dressed. Not even bothering with my wet hair or make up I threw my belongings into my case, prepared to leave. "I heard everything you said!" I shouted out of the window, ran down the stairs, into my car and I was gone. Tears rolled down my face, I cried harder than I had ever cried before. My brother hated me and thought I was a joke; my best friends were not what they seemed and now Fancy Pants was dating some duck-faced woman that looked half my age. Was this book actually fucking my life up?

"God, my fucking life," I screamed out. My phone went off in my bag and I tried to reach it but couldn't. Sitting back up, a rabbit ran out into the road and I tried to do an emergency stop, swerved and hit a rock. Bang. I heard my tyre pop and my car spun around into the middle of the road, hitting my head against the glass. "Fuck!" I screamed out again. "I can't afford a new fucking tyre!"

Jumping out of the car, lightheaded from the bang to my head, I noticed my hand was hurting too; it looked like I had broken my little finger. I was stuck in the middle of nowhere, in the dark. I got back in the car and tried to straighten it up and pulled over to the right side of the road. I sat for a long time and looked out at the stars, crying, not knowing what to do, my head racing with emotions.

Getting out of the car again I stood in silence, then from deep in my gut I screamed at the top of my voice. "Fuck off, all of you! I will never trust anyone again!" Picking up some stones from the floor, trying not to hurt my hand, I threw them into the distance. I needed to lash out, I was filled with anger and disappointment. Falling to the floor in a heap, I gave into my injuries and slowly walked back to the car. My phone was dead, so I couldn't call the AA to come and rescue me. I would have to sit all night in the dark and brave it out until I was found. I searched for a blanket in the boot, wrapped it around myself and examined my head. It was a pretty bad bump. Wrapping tissues around my hand to support my finger, I stared up at the stars. "Goodnight, Fox," I whispered. My lip quivered, and warm tears rolled down my face, before I finally fell asleep.

Chapter Twenty-three:
It Was a Very Good Year

Between the publishers and I we had sent the blurb for the book everywhere. I had called a few radio stations and left messages and luckily, not long after the book was released, BBC Radio Leeds responded and asked me to come on the show to talk about the book. I'd never been so scared in my life. I had no idea what I was going to be asked, and it was completely live and unpractised. Sitting on the train to Leeds, I stared out of the window with my earphones in, when my phone rang, and it was my mother. "Hello, darling, just ringing to wish you luck. I will be tuned in when you are on air. Are you okay?" She sounded exactly the same, as she had the day I was about to take my exams. "Don't say the word 'Fuck' will you, darling; you will let yourself down. Keep it clean," she continued, worrying and fussing for nothing.

"No swearing, I promise," I smiled down into the phone and shook my head.

"Do you look smart? Have you had some breakfast?" Rolling my eyes frustratedly, I replied,

"I'm smart; I'm sober and I'm confident. I've got this, don't worry. I'm pulling into Leeds train station. Look, I will call you after the interview. I promise," I tried to reassure her.

"Good luck, I'm so proud of you!" And with a million kissing sounds, she hung up. The train stopped. I had had no breakfast and I was desperate for a glass of wine to stop my nerves, but I pushed through it and flagged a taxi down.

"Saint Peter's Square, please, the broadcasting centre." I got in the back of the taxi and he set off.

"Are you going to work?" the taxi driver asked.

"No, I'm being interviewed today, by one of the producers. I've written a book," I smiled at him in the mirror.

"Oh, what's it about?" he looked at me excitedly.

"It's a pornographic love story," I said without thinking and bit my lip looking back out of the taxi window.

"Oh, my goodness, well... us northerners like a bit of smut," his eyes gleamed with excitement. "Tell me more, what's it called?" he hit his brakes hard, not concentrating.

"It's called 'A Year of Tiramisu'," I sighed, wishing I'd never started the conversation as we were now stuck in back-to-back traffic.

"So, how rude is it?" he continued. "You don't look the type to write a mucky book; you look so professional and sweet," he leered at me, as though he was undressing me with his mind. I gave him an intimidating stare. He grabbed a newspaper off the seat and placed it over his lap. "We are here. That will be £9.50," he choked, looking uncomfortable and I handed him his fare.

"Keep the change, you, filthy animal," I winked and got out of the cab.

Looking up at the BBC building, the nerves hit me again and I felt a strange sensation as my endorphins kicked in. I walked to the reception area and told them that I was there to do a radio interview, signed in and was given a visitor badge. I was then told to sit and wait on a large leather sofa very similar to the one I had sat on when I first visited Fancy Pants' house. I hated Fancy Pants now and pretty much everyone else in my life. I was full of attitude again after being fucked over by everyone and just wanted to do things my own way again. I'd even pushed the Fox away through fear of rejection and pain. The accident had given me a wakeup call; having used two of my nine lives, now I thought it was best, if I just lived my life to the full and protected what I had, rather than giving a shit about how others viewed me.

"L.J. Brown?" a voice appeared from nowhere and startled me. I turned my head and a dashing young man came to greet me with a warm reassuring smile, reaching out his hand. I shook it and smiled back.

"Hi, you must be Mr. Producer, it's great to finally meet you," I beamed and shook his hand for too long.

"Follow me, I will take you to the studio. Can I get you a coffee?" He was so polite and well spoken, but not at all like I had imagined him in my head.

"Yes, actually I would love one," I said, expecting him to join me. He got a coffee for me and then sat me down in another waiting area.

"We will come and get you five minutes before you are due on air. Are you okay to sit here?" I nodded and started to feel scared of what was to come. It was really happening to me; I was about to go on the radio for the first time in my life.

"I'll be back soon," and dashing through the doors to the studio he was gone, and I was left to wait. Looking around the room I could see photos of all the famous stars that had been into the studio; the Spice girls were on the wall and countless others. I grounded myself and tried to relax, telling myself to 'stop thinking and just do it!' In no time at all the producer was back and he showed me the way to the studio. I walked in and I could hear the radio, live. Sitting behind the glass was a blond lady with a head set on and talking into a microphone, introducing a song. She looked up, beamed a smile at me and waved. I waved back nervously.

"So, in a few minutes you go in. She's just finishing playing a song before you go live. No swearing on air as it's early morning radio. You'll be fine, just be you." That's what I'm afraid of, I thought to myself.

I entered the room and was introduced to the radio presenter who shook my hand and was so lovely to me that I instantly felt at ease. I was then asked to wear the headphones if I felt comfortable, or just speak into the microphone. I decided to just speak into the microphone and before I knew it, we were live on air.

"From Adele, that's 'Someone Like You'. BBC Radio Leeds it's nine forty-five. I'm here until midday. Now... L.J. Brown, Yorkshire author as I have just mentioned before. Her book has been described by the publisher as 'not for the easily offended or faint-hearted' and she joins me this morning. Good morning!"

"Good morning," I answered, terrified.

"I have not read the book, we just got a copy this morning, you've literally arrived in the studio about three or four minutes ago and I opened up on chapter twelve. Just the title of the chapters, I'm like oh my gosh. So for those that like Fifty Shades, this will be right up their street, because Fifty Shades of Grey was a global phenomenon, wasn't it?"

"It was, yes. They are saying it is the next Fifty Shades of Grey, but it's actually a lot ruder," I immediately cringed at my comment. Fuck! I didn't want to sound big headed, but people had been comparing it, although it was nothing like Fifty Shades to me, other than being about sex. Why didn't I say that? Instantly I was a mess and just wanted a hole to swallow me up in the studio floor.

"So did Fifty Shades of Grey inspire you to write this book?" she continued.

"I actually thought that was quite tame, so no it didn't inspire me." I gave a silly laugh that I wouldn't normally have made, and I sounded like a man and… why do I have no filter? "It was true to life, as it was my own experiences and I wrote from the heart so…" I continued. Now shut up, you stupid woman! Cringe factor of a million.

"So, the back story is you were married for fourteen years?"

"I was."

"And I'm guessing you married quite young?"

"I did, yes."

"And after fourteen years of marriage, was it you that said 'that's it' or did it just run its course?"

"I left, due to affairs on both sides. It just got to the stage that we were fighting constantly, and the

kids weren't enjoying being in that environment, so I said, 'Okay, I'm going,' and I left. It was very hard at first, but this amazing book's come out of it, so..."
Fuck, I just admitted to having an affair on the radio... Oh my god, I'm going to throw up! My ex-husband didn't even know that.

"And then you entered into the world of online dating as well?"

"I did... Oh my goodness, I did!" I took a deep breath.

"Oh, it's awful. I'm single also and there are a few sites that I have had a look on and I just think to myself... I don't know... it's the way that guys speak back to you."

"Oh, I know, it's just horrendous." (Where the fuck did that posh voice come from, I thought to myself as I heard it.) I shuddered and told myself to just keep going, I had already made a complete dick out of myself on the radio!

"And then the pictures that you get sent. I'm like... really? Did you have to send that?"

"Yes, there's a whole chapter on the pictures I got sent," I sympathised with her experience.

"Is there?"

"Yeah, like sixty-four of them!" I looked at her and told her with my eyes that I was used to it by now.

"Sixty-four of them," she gasped, and I giggled. I was now starting to relax with her, and it felt like I had known her ages and we were connected, like the millions of other listeners probably would be to similar experiences. "So literally you start chatting away and within about three or four exchanges, then comes the picture and you're like, why? Why do you feel the need?"

"Yeah, it's so sleazy. It's like, that really makes me want to go on a date with you, doesn't it?" I jested with her and laughed.

"But the whole world of online dating has totally changed things, hasn't it? When I first started going out in the '90's, you'd just meet people in bars," she said, matter of factly.

"Yes, that's how I met my husband, just by social interaction." I cringed again... For fuck's sake, shut up, I thought to myself... and stop talking over her... just answer the question without rushing your thoughts. My heart began to pound, and I felt sick again; I was totally screwing this up.

"Whereas now it's Tinder, Plenty of Fish..."

"Plenty of freaks!" I blurted out.

"Yeah, plenty of freaks." Thankfully she laughed. "And so, I'm guessing a lot of the online dating falls into this book, which is called A Year of Tiramisu."

"Yes, it's called that because that's what I stuff my face with every time I get dumped," I said quite clearly now, trying to bring things back around, starting to sound reasonably okay and confident.

"How many dates did you go on? How many times did you get dumped?" She sounded surprised.

"I went on over a hundred dates in a year." She gasped in shock at the comment. "I went on three in one day once; breakfast, dinner and tea." I was giggling a lot now and getting into the flow and relaxing.

"Okay!" You could tell she was thinking, 'omg what are you doing going on that many dates?'

"I kind of knew after about five minutes if they were a complete weirdo and I escaped out of a lot of fire escapes." Talking over her again, I announced that I had got stuck in a window once, trying to escape from a date. "Honestly I was just like run for the hills!" I giggled again into the microphone.

"If I'm honest, I have looked at hotel bars or restaurants and you do look at the window in the toilet and think, can I fit through that?"

"Exactly," I smiled at her, giggling.

"It does enter your mind, doesn't it, when you just think... this is not going great."

"That's the first thing I look for when I go on a date... where can I escape." I nodded in agreement. "When did you get stuck; where was it?"

I froze to the spot because not only could I not remember the restaurant name, I knew I'd been told to not give too much away for legal reasons and it already wasn't going too well. "Ermm... it was, oh I can't remember the restaurant name now, but it was in Leeds and we'd decided on an Italian. I had gone on this date with a lawyer. We had been talking on POF for a couple of weeks."

"Which is short for Plenty of Fish?" she confirmed with me.

"Yeah, and he was really nice. The conversation was great, but I didn't see many pictures of him, so I just went with my instincts. I thought it's going to be okay, he's got a good job, seems to have everything together. So, I met him in this restaurant, and he texted saying *I'm already sat down at the table*. I thought to myself that's strange, but the closer I got to the table, the more I realised that this guy was possibly just under five feet and on his profile, he had put that he was six feet two!" She snorted a little laugh. "So, I was sitting with this guy and everyone was looking at me because I'm six feet when I have my heels on and, well, everyone was just laughing. I thought to myself Oh my goodness, please no. But towards the end of the evening, I just got horribly drunk."

"On tiramisu?"

"Yes, on tiramisu..." I laughed at the smart reference.

"I got horribly drunk because I had to and the guy got really suggestive, so I was trying to talk to him about friendship and how important it is at the beginning of a relationship and before I knew it, he had his pants down underneath the table and he put my hand…"

She broke me off before I could go any further into the description of my experience. "No… No!" She shook her head, as if to say, 'don't say anything else'. Shocked and amused at the same time, I pursed my lips. "Goodness me, well, bearing in mind it's nine fifty-five in the morning… So, this book…" she changed the subject quickly. "Where did the inspiration come to write it? So, it wasn't Fifty Shades that inspired you; did you just think, I've got all these stories and been on all of these dates and done all of these things, wouldn't it be kind of good to document it all?"

"Yes, well I also wanted to warn women about the pitfalls and the dangers, because I'd been in such tricky situations that the police were called out to me on one date… you read about it… I wanted people to know that it's very, very not safe out there…" Oh shit, I can't even speak the Queens English now. "Unsafe, not, not safe!" Cringe moment again… my poor family! "So that was one of the main messages for this book," I continued, "but I fell deeply in love with someone I met on POF, so it's a love story as well I suppose." Tears were starting to well in my eyes, as I was overwhelmed by the feelings I had experienced for him.

"And was it unrequited?" she asked, reading me, looking sad for me.

"Yes, he didn't give a ... No, not at all, and I chased him around because I really did fall for him terribly and I couldn't see the wood for the trees. So, yes, it's my love story. I guess I wrote it for him in a way, but I wanted to also put the message across to people that it's a real jungle out there and to be careful!" I pulled myself together, feeling strong again. "You do have to be careful, especially women as well. But also, I think for both sides these days, when you are just meeting people on apps, you don't know who you're meeting. I mean you have no idea." I started talking over her again, too eager to put my point across. "I know I've been on loads of dates and then found out that people were married, so I'd go and have a look on their Facebook, Instagram, etc. and there's a picture of them and their wife and I'd just snogged them. I'm like 'Oh my goodness!' The internet is full of lies, I thought to myself."

"Oh, gosh," she sighed. "And this is going global as well, because you're getting people all over the world buying it?"

"Yes, it's all over the world and in a few different languages now. It's in Barnes & Noble in

America; it's in Waterstones and it's also on Amazon. It's got some good reviews. Yes, it's gone crazy. I feel very lucky and it's only been out a month."

"You're joking…" she sounded surprised.

"Nope, a month," I affirmed.

"So, there is an explicit warning on the back that even Fifty Shades didn't have," she observed, looking at the book again.

"I know right, there's lots of swearing too, but the worst thing is my mum picked up a copy and read it!" I covered my face and laughed.

"Oh gosh… and what did she say?"

"She said, 'You are grounded for the rest of your life and I'm buying you a chastity belt!" We both howled with laughter.

"So, it's called A Year of Tiramisu. If you like something that is a little bit raunchy and a little bit risky, oh chapter five, 'Naked dancing'…"

"Oh yes, there's lots of naked dancing in the book." I smiled at her in amusement.

"Let's just go through some of the chapter names… Chapter six, 'Marriage should be made illegal'?"

"Yes, I strongly disagree with marriage now. I'll never get married again…" ('unless the Fox asks me by a miracle,' I thought to myself and shook the feeling off faster than I had thought it).

"So…ever? The guy that you met, that you fell head over heels in love with… Okay, so if you get that again and he feels the same way about you… you'll get married again?"

'Maybe,' I thought to myself, but wanted to stick to my original plan of never letting anyone get that close again. "No, I don't believe in it anymore." I said unconvincingly.

"Really? Oh gosh, I can't read chapter seven's title! I'll show it to you." She showed me, and I burst into laughter after she'd opened it on 'Blow Jobs and Bottoms'. "But, if you do want a bit of filth in your life, A Year of Tiramisu by L.J. Brown is available in all good book shops and online as well. And you know what, this has got a film written all over it! I can't read chapter sixteen's title either," she looked shocked and amused both at the same time. "L.J. Brown, thank you for coming in this morning. When you do an interview like this, because the book is quite raunchy, there is so much you want to say on the air but you just can't do it because it's not past the radio watershed it's ten past ten in the morning and you just have to be so careful. But if you are a fan of raunchy novels, it's available now: 'A Year of Tiramisu'. It's going worldwide, and it was born here in Yorkshire. Thank you so much for coming L.J., it's been great to meet you."

"Thank you for having me," I said gratefully.

"You're welcome." And we had finished the interview.

She pulled her head set off, smiled at me and told me I did well. I was shaking with the adrenaline and thanked her so much for her time, signing her book, writing, '*Here's a book of fucking filth*'. I grabbed my bag and gave her a firm handshake goodbye. The producer was waiting outside the studio with my coat.

"Oh my god, did I do okay? I think I messed it up, I was so nervous."

"You came across fine, don't worry," he said reassuringly. "What are you going to do now?"

"I'm off to the pub. I need a good stiff drink!" Thinking that I'd made an idiot out of myself on the radio, I thought I deserved to get a little drunk. I had seven missed calls: six from my family and one message from the Fox. "You nailed it, young lady, well done! Call me when you are free."

I reached the train station bar, ordered a large glass of red and sank into a chair, dialling his number. "So did my sexy Yorkshire accent turn you on, Fox? Did you get a hardon?" I laughed down the phone and we talked for hours.

Chapter Twenty-four:
One for My Baby and One More for the Road

Since the radio interview, my life had become a whirlwind of chaos. All the people that knew who I was had either congratulated me immensely for merely publishing a book or had turned against me, and it seemed like my circle of those I could trust or relate to was getting smaller and smaller. I had to come off social media and as a result of the stress I was snapping at the Fox and verbally giving him black eyes when I was drunk. My drinking had become a problem; I was waking up in the morning wanting wine instead of coffee. I couldn't sleep or eat, and I was becoming depressed. Arriving at work, I got my head down and focused on the only thing I seemed to have control of. I was good, really good at this job. I was top biller and I loved what I did.

Work was going great, apart from the people I worked with, who had changed their behaviour towards me since the radio interview. I had a meeting with my new manager to discussed how things were going. "So, everything is going well. Your figures are fine, and you have hit all your targets," he gave me a reassuring smile.

"But no one talks to me in the office. I'm ignored half of the time, spoken to like shit the rest of the time. What's everyone's problem? I'm nothing but nice to people." I bobbed my head trying not to cry.

"You openly admitted to having an affair and putting your hand on a man's cock in a restaurant, on local radio L.J. It doesn't sit well with everyone."

"I didn't put my hand on his cock; he put my hand on his cock. And my ex-husband had an affair first; I just got my own back," I said, frustrated that the facts were not correct.

"People never like it when you are doing well. You're hitting all your targets and you are an author, and potentially going to make money from your book. I suppose people don't know why you're even here." He shrugged his shoulders and I could tell he didn't give a shit if I was there or not.

"I have a family to feed and support like everyone else. Of course, I have to work," I looked at him like he was stupid.

"When do you get your royalties?"

"In five months' time. Every six months money just goes into my account, but I might not make anything, I have no idea how sales are doing, I don't get a big cut, the publishers take most of it." I rushed my words out and gathered my things off the table, knowing I had a call soon with a client.

"Look, just get your head down. It's like school; you can't always be popular," he tried to be sympathetic but failed.

"It shouldn't be like fucking school. It's a professional company; shit like this shouldn't happen." I hissed, suffering from a hangover and knowing I had to call the Fox later to apologise for a fight I had caused between us, after a bottle of wine and a bad day.

"Miss Saggy Tits over there tried to impersonate me, taking the piss out of my book openly in front of the whole office and you as well as everyone else just laughed." I looked at him red faced.

"You brought it on yourself. You should have just kept your mouth shut and not told anyone. Anyway, you laughed too," he barked at me.

"I had no choice; everyone else was. I love my job, but I hate working here. I'm going to have to consider my options," I said assertively, getting up and walking towards the door. "Whatever way you look at it I'm being bullied at work." I opened the door and bolted out. Fighting my tears, I sat back down at my desk and I could see everyone looking at me. I got on the phone, called my client and got on with my day.

Time flew by and I was out of the office before I knew it. I got in my car and dialled the Fox to apologise. "L.J.," he answered, reserved.

"Look, Fox, I'm sorry. I didn't mean to be so out of order; I have a lot going on." I tried to be as gentle with my delivery as possible. "My life's falling apart, and I was drunk and didn't know what I was saying." I looked at myself in the mirror and saw the bags under my eyes from not sleeping.

"You were so aggressive L.J. I won't be spoken to like that by anyone," he said without feeling.

"Fox, you know how much you mean to me; you are my best friend! I don't know what I'd do without you in my life, but I understand if you don't want this anymore." I bit my lip and hoped he wouldn't agree.

"You need to stop drinking. It's awful when you are drunk, and I don't like it. I grew up with a father that drank."

I paused and my heart sank. I'm sorry, Fox. Please give me another chance; I need you!" 'I love you,' I thought to myself, alarmed. "I will go and see a doctor and get some help. I need to sleep; I feel so tired and ill," I said, exhausted. He was silent. "I signed for my new house by the way. I get the keys at the weekend and I don't have the kids. How about I answer the door naked?" I tried to raise some heat, but he still remained quiet.

"I'll come over and we can talk, but in the meantime, sort yourself out, young lady," he said with conviction and hung up.

Fuck my life… things were supposed to get better, not worse, and do have a drinking problem? How am I supposed to sort that out? Overwhelmed, I pulled up outside the children's school and tried to collect my emotions so that they didn't know I was upset. Putting a fake smile on my face, I pretended everything was okay and got out of the car.

Chapter Twenty-five:
High Hopes

Signing the paperwork for my new house was like a dream come true. The house was immaculate, detached and in a nice part of town. It had a small private garden, and the best part was the underfloor heating. Signing my life away, I was handed the keys and we shook hands. I left the office with a massive grin. Getting in my car, I called my best friend, the only person who had truly stuck with me since I was a little girl, no matter what happened in my life. "Beth, I got the keys!" I screamed at her excitedly. "Wait until you see it, you'll love it!"

"I'm so pleased for you, hun. Are you still coming over later today? I know you said you really needed to talk about something," she said comforting me.

"If you're sure you don't mind me talking about men?" I said exasperated with myself.

"And your health, I'm worried about all this stress you're under. We will sit down and work it all out. Look, I have to go. Get your glad rags on and I'll see you at seven p.m.," and she hung up. I arrived at the old house, now terrified of living there, because I never knew what was going to happen next. I had become used to putting headphones on so I couldn't hear anything that was happening; it was an awful way to have to live. Now I could see the end to my suffering, only these mountains of boxes between me and freedom. I spent a few hours manically packing up, cleaning and trying to make sure I had done everything, before going away for the night. Opening my fridge, I took out a salad and some potatoes and started to prepare dinner. Chopping into the cucumber, I had a flashback of the Fox and stopped in my tracks, smiling.

Grabbing my phone, I took a photo of the cucumber and added '*I was making dinner and thought of you*' with a wink and blush and sent it to the Fox. Immediately he replied: '*Naughty girl!*' I smiled widely and continued to chop the salad, then decided to take another photo. I dropped my top to the floor and took a photo of my breasts with my nipples hard from the cold, bit my lip and sent it. '*Mmmmm… beautiful*,' he replied, and I instantly wanted him to be with me.

Then he called. "Is it cold in Yorkshire?" he asked wickedly.

"It wouldn't be cold if your body was against mine!"

Putting the knife down, I gave him my full attention. "Shall I go to the bedroom, you, sexy fucker for some phone sex?" I started to touch my breasts and feel aroused by his voice.

"Nope, sorry, I have to go," and he hung up.

I was shocked and confused so called him right back. "Fox? Erm... I don't understand?" I asked, confused.

"I was just joking with you, L.J., but I do actually have to go; I have football. I'll be seeing you tomorrow anyway, won't I?"

"Yes, you have my new address. Text me when you're on the way." I sounded fed up. I was missing him so much.

"I'll see you then. Are you okay? It's good to see you're eating. Make sure you are okay tonight. Don't drink too much," he continued, knowing me so well by now that he could see the pitfalls of a night out before they happened.

"I'm with my best mate and she doesn't drink. I will be okay." I secretly loved it that he watched out for me.

"Have a great time. I must go. I'm sorry... see you tomorrow," he paused and so did I, not wanting to leave each other.

"Bye Fox," I said miserably. It was getting so hard being apart; I was missing him all the time now.

"Goodbye, young lady." And we both rang off.

Biting a slice of cucumber, I snorted a laugh, pulled myself together and began getting ready for my night out. Looking at my body in the full-length mirror, I noticed that I had added a few pounds; my breasts had become larger and my bottom had more shape. My face was glowing, and my hair had become shiny. I looked healthy, not frail and thin. I was happy and I had started eating and sleeping much better than I had done in years. I felt like I was becoming content, or just finally accepting that I couldn't carry on abusing my body with fags, booze and late nights anymore.

My choice of clothes had always been a selection of short dresses, or tight trousers and heels. I decided to put on a pair of casual jeans, some flat shoes and a nice top. I didn't need to impress anyone anymore. I looked good and I didn't need to shout 'hey look at me!' to the world anymore. The only person I wanted to look at me was my beautiful Silver Fox.

Arriving in my hometown, I pulled up outside my friend's house and the door was immediately opened. "Aww babes, it's great to see you. You look amazing, so well!" She hugged me and gave me a kiss.

"I feel good, really good. I'm sorry for crying on the phone the other day. I'm just a bit overwhelmed by this guy I've met. I need to talk, that's all."

"I can talk all night, L.J. Let's go buy a fucking big steak and chips though; I'm starving to death!" Her mouth was watering at the idea.

"Oh, fuck yes, steak, chips and a glass of wine! Well, pop for you." I was still getting used to her being teetotal. I looked up the road and got a shiver.

"What is it, L.J?" she looked concerned.

"I just saw my old house out of the corner of my eye, and it made my stomach turn." I looked at her and she was sympathetic.

"Well, just look how far you have come since then. Don't look at it," and she dragged me into the house. "So, what's been going on? Last I heard you were still hung up on that dickhead Fancy Pants." She poured me a glass of pop and started to roll a cigarette.

"Oh, he was contacting me for ages off and on, usually because he was responding to my messages, but he was sending sexting messages right up until he announced he was with some girl. I have no idea who she is, but she looks a bit like a duck. I'm such a bitch. I'm sure she's a nice girl." I snorted into my glass.

"Let me see a photo of him. You know I'm sure I saw him in town a few weeks ago, but he was with a much older woman. Is he Italian?"

"It was probably his mother; she lives here," I cringed.

"Ha, what are the chances; so does your mum! I wonder if they have coffee mornings together?" She laughed at the thought.

"I don't have Facebook since all this shit with the book, so I can't show you a photo I'm afraid." She then grabbed her phone and had a look for him on her Facebook. It took her a while and then she found him.

"He looks like a right bell-end. What were you thinking?" She showed me a photo of him with Duckface, looking happy, and I looked away, still not sure what I was feeling about the situation.

"Well, he's no longer my problem; he's hers," I said with conviction.

"Glad to hear it. He treated you like shit. I have never seen you fall apart so badly; he's not good for you and not worth your time." She smiled at me, busy typing away.

"What are you doing?" I questioned her.

"I've just written a comment on his Facebook relationship status, so the world knows he's a cheating wanker and giant cockhead and that I feel sorry for poor Duckface. She literally doesn't know what she's letting herself in for." Beth was bold and honest at the best of times and a very over-protective friend.

"Now, L.J., the fucker will work out where it's come from and never come near you again!"

She grabbed me and squeezed me hard. "Fuck! Oh no, Beth, he will kill me, kill you!" I panicked as I would never have had the guts to do anything like that. "Can't you take it down? It's not the right thing to do. What if you get in trouble?" I was grateful for her support but knew how dark Fancy Pants could be. "Take it down, Steph. Honestly, he's not even worth it." I grabbed her phone and tried to go on to delete the message, but someone was already typing a comment on it, then his Facebook had gone on to lock down and no more comments could be made and she was blocked. "Oh my god, he's jumped on it immediately," I said, feeling sick, looking at her wide eyed.

"I did it, L.J., not you and I'm glad. I'm not scared of the fucking tosser. If he wasn't guilty, he wouldn't have reacted that way; he would have stuck up for himself. Says it all really. Karma's a bitch! Anyone that hurts you, I will go after." She grabbed her bag and took her phone and mine and put them in her top drawer.

"Let's leave the phones here and go out and talk. She grabbed my hand and pulled me out of the door before I could object, and we were on route to the train station.

"Two return tickets to Leeds, please," I said, paying for them. Boarding the train, we had to stand up all the way, as everyone seemed to have had the same idea. "God, how busy is it?" It was full of teenagers, drunk and loud, and I looked at them and remembered my youth and how much fun I used to have doing the same thing. My age was starting to finally hit me.

"Stop thinking about the message. We are out to enjoy ourselves!" She grabbed my face and squeezed it, making my cheeks look fat. I took a deep breath and thought to myself, 'Well, it had only been on for seconds, he would have got rid of it without anyone seeing it, I'm sure it wouldn't have done any harm.'

"So, this new guy. He seems to have quite a calming effect on you. Tell me about him." I smiled and went deep into thought.

"I met him through work. I was trying to help him find a job, but then ended up helping him recruit for his company. He became a friend and talked to me for months about Fancy Pants, before I even snogged him." I light up with the memory of the kiss in the lift.

"How long have you been seeing him for?"

"About eight months." I screwed my face up, knowing what was coming next.

"Eight months and you have only just told me?" She sounded shocked.

"Well, it's complicated. He lives really far away, and I said to him in the beginning, no feelings, just sex. At that point I really didn't want my heart to be hurt again, so I just wanted to have fun."

She rolled her eyes, looked mad. "I get it that you got hurt, but you tell a guy that and that's all they will want from you!" She shook her head.

"He's not like that." I began to instinctively protect him. "Don't get me wrong, we do have a lot of sex," I began to whisper as there were people next to us on the train.

"If he has you at his beck and call, L.J., he's no better than Fancy Pants." She was starting to get mad with me, because I couldn't see her point of view.

"We go out for dinner; we talk for hours; he supports me, and he even asks about the children. He puts hours of time into making sure I am safe and well and eating. Honestly, he's absolutely nothing like Fancy Pants. He is not a bastard. He never ignores me or blocks me; he always replies, and he travels halfway up the country on a regular basis to be with me whenever he can. That's serious effort."

"So, has he told you how he feels about you; what his plans are?" she probed further.

"No, we just enjoy the moments we have together. They are always amazing, and I literally can't wait to hear his voice every day." I started to feel a longing for him and felt sad.

"So, are you in love? Is he in love with you?" I looked at her, terrified.

"Yes, I am, deeply." A tear welled up in my eye and she punched me on the shoulder.

"Keep it together, lass." I pursed my lips and stood tall. "Well then, don't you think you need to tell him? Eight months is a long time to be shagging and not talk about feelings. Worst thing that can happen is he says he doesn't feel the same and then you can move on."

"Move on? Why am I moving on?" I felt sick at the idea of never having anything to do with him again, like it would be literally impossible to let him go. "When he looks at me, I only ever see his eyes. It's like he's so far inside my head, that I'm talking to his soul." I had feelings about wanting to be a mum again and marriage and I never thought I'd ever want any of those things. I found myself daydreaming about all the possibilities, trying to keep my hopes high.

"Well, I have to say, I have not seen you in love before; it's really nice and refreshing to see. I hope for your sake that the feelings are mutual, but I'm here for you if they are not, okay?"

She looked out of the train window. "Come on, let's go get that steak. I've got a lot to tell you too." Getting off the train she suddenly jumped onto a bench nearby and stood up tall and bold. "Can I have your attention please, everyone?" she shouted loudly, turning everyone's heads, "I just want to tell you all that this lovely lady in front of me has finally fallen in love!"

Laughing and clapping she jumped back down, as pissed people all around me started to cheer and clap, patting me on the back.

"Steph, I'm going to kill you," I blushed and glared at her lovingly, as she followed behind me, doubled up in laughter and clapping with everyone else.

"Hahaha… you should have seen your face! See, life's pretty fucking awesome L.J. You need to smile and be happy! And tell him you love him!"

Chapter Twenty-six:
I Can't Believe I'm Losing You

I opened the door to my new house; it was completely empty. I walked around every room thinking about where everything would go and became stupidly excited. It smelt new. No damp, no noise, just a perfect space for me and the kids. I'd picked up a bottle of wine and something sexy to wear for the arrival of the Fox. I went upstairs to the bathroom and got changed. I'd decided to wear a Sinatra hat, a white shirt left unbuttoned and some black heels, with no panties or bra. I texted him to say I was here and waiting with the door unlocked and just to come in.

The only items in the kitchen were two wine glasses, the bottle and a small gift box. I had bought him a little something to help me focus on talking to him about my feelings and not letting myself avoid telling him I was ready to commit to him. I had tried to plan out what I was going to say in my head a million times and needed a drink to help me have the confidence to follow it through.

"Hello." I could hear his voice as he opened the door.

"I'm in the kitchen," I shouted, and my heart started to race.

"Oh my god... nice hat," he gasped at me and rushed to my lips to kiss me, knocking my hat off. Standing back from me, he just looked at me and I felt like I was the most beautiful woman alive.

"Wine?" I asked, smirking at him.

"I think I'll drink your pussy first," he said, lowering himself to the floor and kissing me in between my legs. Sticking his fingers deep inside me and rolling his tongue around, he sucked me hard, not letting me move. I took a sip of wine and started to moan. I closed my eyes and let him work his magic. Opening them again, I could see that he was watching me intently and he went harder and deeper.

"I'm going to cum!" I screamed out, warning him. I came so hard that I gushed out, soaking the floor and him. He picked me up and put me on the sink top, that had never been used. Dropping his pants and pulling my shirt off, we kissed, and he thrust himself inside me. I lost balance and laughed into his mouth. We were both now looking into each other eyes, close to coming together.

"Stop!" I ordered assertively, and he pulled out.

"What's the matter?" He looked confused.

"I want to do something to you." I grabbed his hand in mine and walked upstairs, him following behind me. I could feel his eyes watching my naked body. I took him to my room which was empty. "This is where the bed will go," I bounced around animated, "so stand about here," I instructed him, and he looked amused. I dropped to my knees and looked up at him.

"You have a nice place, L.J. I like it." He sounded impressed.

"Don't stop me," I said to him seductively and he knew what I was about to do.

Putting his hard cock in my mouth I began to suck it slowly, gently and deeply, building up the motion, grabbing his balls in my hand. His legs began to stiffen and his breaths shorten, I could see that he was close, so I stopped and put one of his balls in my mouth and sucked it gently, licking the inside of his leg and then took his cock back into my mouth. I got back into a slow rhythm and then put my hands on his ass and pounded his cock into the back of my throat a few times, nearly gagging, but staying in complete control.

"L.J., I'm going to cum," he said, trying to pull away, but I locked him to me so he couldn't escape. He made a noise I had never heard before, an aching moan that went on for a few seconds and his eyes burned into mine, as he watched me swallow him and enjoy it.

"L.J., no one's ever made me cum that way before," he said, falling to his knees slowly and holding me; his energy was sapped. "God, I thought I would never stop; I came for so long," he looked dazed and confused.

"I need to get a drink. Come downstairs?" I pulled him up and we kissed, then walked together to refresh ourselves. I refilled the glasses and looked at the box on the side and he followed my eyes. "I have a little gift for you," I said shyly and gestured that the box was for him. Picking it up, I passed it to him and waited for his response.

"It's a key," he said, confused.

"It's a key to the house. I want you to be able to come and go as you please, especially if I'm at work and the kids are at their dad's. You can just let yourself in without waiting around for me." I couldn't tell him it was commitment; I was still terrified.

"Wow, well thank you. The only person that's ever given me a key to their house is my mum," he beamed at me and I felt safe that it was okay, and he hadn't freaked out. We started to kiss again, and he was hard, so I played with him while he talked to me about his plans for the day and ideas for the house.

"L.J., I'm ready to go again." He flipped me over and pulled my hair back. Inside me once more, he was fucking me against the wall, hard and fast. "You

221

are perfect; you have such an amazing body," he whispered in my ear. "I want to fuck you in every room of this house," he pulled me up against his body and eased himself out, pushing me down onto my back to the floor. With him on top of me, we could feel the underfloor heating and giggled.

I pushed him onto his back and sat on him. With my feet flat to the floor and my body raised, I put his cock back inside me and hovered over him, so he could watch his cock go in and out, picking up speed slowly and just watching him fall apart in front of me. My legs were shaking, and my breasts were bouncing around. "Fuck me, Fox," I said to him with direction. He looked at me, his wicked smile was gone and replaced with an intense stare.

"Get up and come with me," he ordered, leading me back upstairs to the landing. He stopped at the window.

"What are you doing?" I looked at him, shocked, as he faced me towards the window and bent me over. He slowly put his cock into my ass and gently picked up rhythm. I tried to move away from the window, but he put me back.

"People might be able to see us, Fox," I said, half moaning, as he had started to play with my pussy with one hand, putting his fingers inside me and teasing me. Pushing my legs apart he went deeper and deeper and I was screaming out louder than I ever had

before, putting his hand over my mouth, he came inside me, and I flowed, drenching us both in cum...
"I love you!" I shouted out in pleasure, not even thinking about what I was doing, dizzy and out of breath. All I wanted to do was fall into his arms and sleep.

"Can I use your shower?" he said coldly. I stood up and nodded to him in a daze.

"It's just in there, but I only have one towel here and no soap, apart from hand wash." I felt embarrassed about what I had just said. "Look, I'm sorry I said I love you." I turned the shower on for him and watched him get in.

"You lied to me L.J. You said you just wanted fun, that you were in control." I walked away from him and went downstairs to get my wine and come back up to talk to him.

"I've been feeling like this for some time. I want more than just shagging. Don't get me wrong, we have the most amazing time, but I want to explore more with you; I want to be with you." I dropped my head into my hands, then looked at him. "I am in love with you. Fox, don't you feel the same way?" He turned the shower off and got out, drying himself with the towel whilst trying not to look at me. He then gathered his things that were scattered all around the house. He dashed from one room to the next manically desperate to leave the house. His phone began to ring, and he ignored it.

"Who's that calling you?" I glanced at his phone seeing a woman's name and instantly felt dread. "Is there someone else; are you married?" "Fox, we are normally always, completely on the same page. Talk to me."

"L.J., we are not even in the same book. I have told you before. I have a blackness in my heart and I don't have feelings for anyone other than my children. You know this; I have always been clear, and I have never told you I loved you."

"You don't have a black heart. You saved me; without you I'd be dead." I started to cry and reached for my cigarette packet. Not only did he not love me, but it had happened again just like it had with Fancy Pants.

"God doesn't let angels die, L.J. Goodbye and don't smoke; it doesn't suit you." He took one last look at me, dropped eye contact, opened the front door and slammed it behind him sending chills right through me, and he was gone.

I stared into space for what seemed forever, then my legs gave way, and I could feel my heart snap. I slumped to the floor and began to sob uncontrollably. He didn't love me, or was he just fucked up? How could I be so stupid as to not see that I was being used for sex again? I had so many questions left unanswered. How was I supposed to deal with more rejection, and most importantly why was he unable to love me or anyone?

A narcissist and now this? Why do I attract people that don't want me, I thought to myself bewildered?

My phone started to ring, I wiped my eyes, staring at an unknown number calling me. I ignored it and left it to go to answer phone. Shaking I dialled my voicemail, laying back down on the floor continuing to sob. An angry familiar voice filled the room. "L.J. its Fancy Pants, we need to talk. URGENTLY! Call me back!"

To be continued